Hard Ruck

Ruck Boys
Book 2

Maggie Alabaster

Trigger Warnings

Torture (not of a main character).
Kidnapping.
CNC.
Blood play.

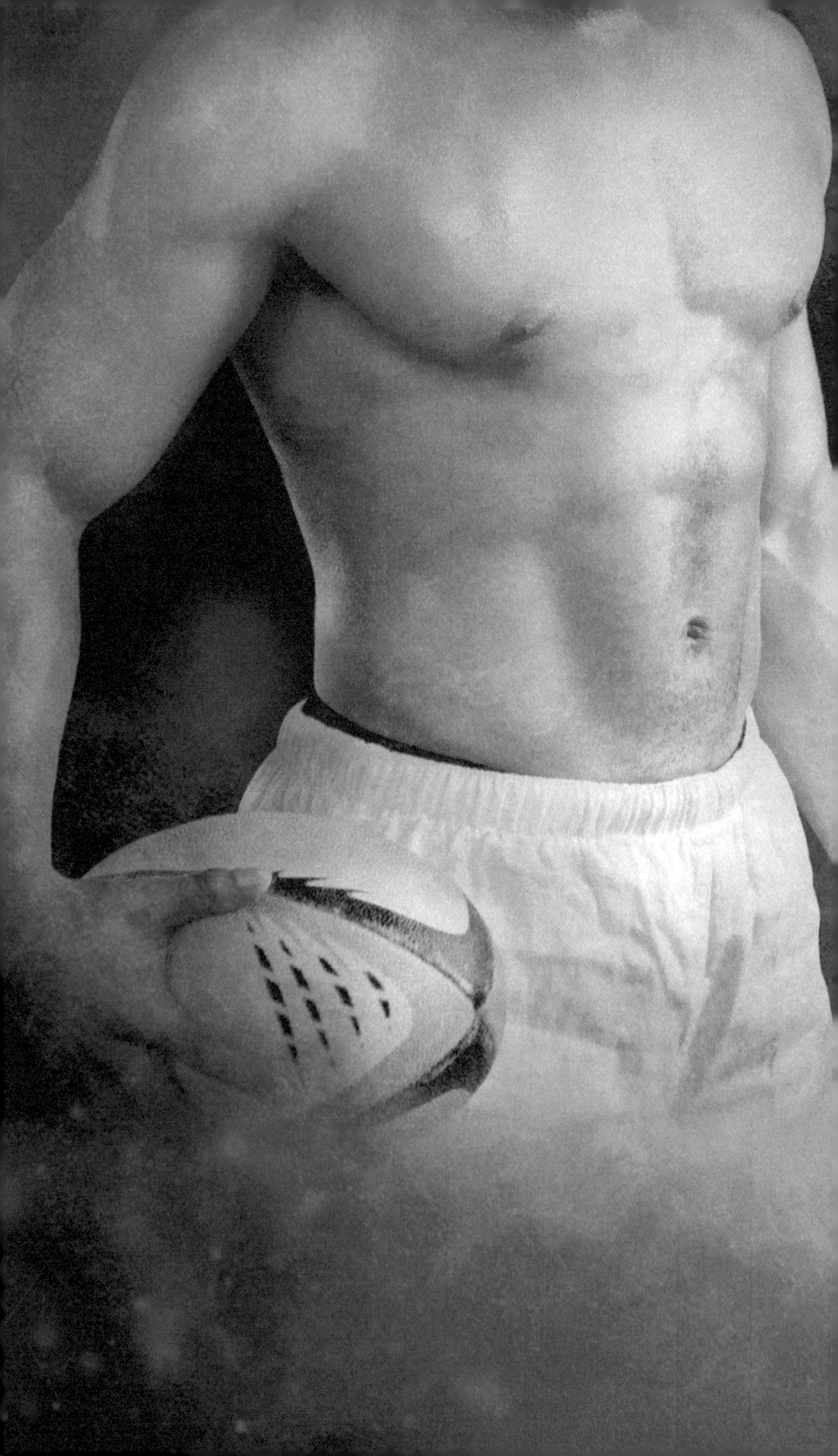

Chapter One

Chelsea

"You're out of your mind." Belinda Simmons's gaze held a rapidly dwindling hint of defiance. There was no heat behind her words now. No anger. Fear was taking over.

I'd watched for the last hour as the fury faded out of her, and she finally realised she was fucked. It should have been satisfying, but it wasn't. Nothing about this was right.

"All I asked was for you to delete that article." I toyed with the gun in my hand. I wouldn't use it, not on her. I didn't need to. I made my point back at her apartment. Her keyboard was shot apart, nothing more than splinters of plastic and wires. Her monitor too. Neither of my bullets had touched her.

She might come to wish they had.

"Who is she?"

I glanced over my shoulder to see my brother reach the bottom step of the stairs that led into his workroom. He handed me a cup of coffee and took the gun from my fingers.

"Belinda Simmons," I said, my tone clipped, controlled. Clinical. "She writes for one of those online magazines that thrive on gossip about famous people."

"Ah." He placed the gun aside and leaned his hip against a stainless steel workbench, his ankles crossed. He sipped his coffee and watched the woman currently chained to the ceiling, both arms raised over her head.

Belinda looked at him with something like hope in her eyes. "There's been some kind of misunderstanding. Whatever this woman thinks is going on—" She jerked her head towards me. "She shot at me and then forced me into the back of her car at gunpoint. She brought me here." Her voice grew increasingly higher with each word. The last two were delivered in a painful shriek.

"Huh, Chelsea did that?" He looked over at me, eyebrows raised in semi-mock disbelief. Most of it was for Belinda's benefit. "I thought you didn't like this shit?"

"I don't," I said dryly. "I made an exception for her."

"See, she admits it," Belinda said. "She's out of her mind. She needs professional help. A doctor."

He smiled just slightly. He didn't take his eyes off me as he responded to her. "As it happens, I'm a doctor."

She sagged slightly, visibly relieved. "Then you can—"

He turned to her, slow and deliberate. "You're misunderstanding. I'm not *that* kind of doctor. Let me introduce myself. Isaac Miller. Most people call me Ice." He was still smiling, but his tone was borderline menacing. "I'm a pathologist. Some people might say I'm pathological, but that's another story. Mostly I work on dead people." He sipped his coffee like he was having a pleasant chat with a friend.

"Sometimes those dead people are alive when they get to me. By 'sometimes,' I mean about ninety-five percent of the time. Once in a while they walk out of here alive, but they usually aren't people who said my sister was out of her mind." He glanced back quickly and gave me a fond smile.

I returned it and gulped my too-hot coffee while watching his words sink into Belinda's mind. I saw the exact moment she realised she might not get out of here alive.

"I've been called worse," I said. I didn't elaborate. That didn't matter right now.

"No one insults my sister and gets away with it." Ice snaked an arm around me and pulled me in to press a kiss to my cheek.

I leaned into him, absorbing his comforting warmth. Only a handful of years older than me, he always looked out for me. Nothing ever seemed to be too much trouble for him where I was concerned.

Some people might find the protective older brother thing annoying or oppressive, but I basked in it. I loved that we still had a close relationship, even as adults. Even with vastly different, separate lives. He had a girlfriend, boyfriend and another partner involved in the relationship, but he always made time for me.

"I spoke rashly," Belinda said quickly. Her thoughts couldn't have been clearer. She thought we were *both* out of our minds. "If you let me go now, I won't say anything to anyone. I'll forget I ever met either of you." She was quickly becoming desperate. Fear began to override rational thought. How long would it take for her to snap?

Ice winced playfully. "That's not nice. How

could you forget us? I thought we were friends, Belinda?"

She gaped at him, struggling to figure out the right words. What could she say that would make us unchain her and let her go? As if the perfect plea and tone would placate us somehow.

"What do you want?" she asked cautiously.

"Ah, the third stage of grief," Ice said with a knowing nod. "Bargaining. One of my favourite stages. Although, depression and acceptance are also good. And I have to give a nod to denial and anger as well. I've seen all of them in here over the years. Can you guess where bargaining gets most people, Chels?"

"Nowhere?" I suggested.

He grinned. "You always were my smartest sister." He gave me another squeeze before stepping away. "She's right; nowhere. One of my interests is testing human endurance. Specifically, how long a person can tolerate pain. It's fascinating. And all for science, of course."

"Of course," I said. I suspected Belinda's tolerance was low. She looked close to pissing herself. I had to give her credit for not doing it already. "I am your only sister though."

He chuckled at the feigned annoyance on my

face. He knew how to get a rise out of me, but he never meant any harm by it. He'd chain himself up in here and torture himself before he did anything to hurt me. Although, he'd enjoy doing that to himself, so it might defeat the purpose.

"You can't just chain someone away in a basement and..." She struggled, trying to pull her wrist out of the cuffs they were in. "When the police catch up to you—"

Ice laughed. "I see you don't know how things work here in Dusk Bay. The police don't have that much influence. They aren't allowed to. Other forces have authority in this city. I'd tell you, but then I'd have to kill you." His brow creased briefly before he smiled again. "Since I'm doing that anyway, Reuben Brantley is the boss around here. Samuel Bell too, to some extent. That's all getting muddy these days, what with Sam's daughter being with Reuben's brothers?" He waved his coffee cup in the air dismissively.

"But the Brantley family is involved in..." Belinda's eyes widened. "Organised crime. That's what you are, isn't it? That's why you think you can do this and get away with it."

She struggled again.

Ice laughed. "I can't just get away with it, I'm

paid to do this. I have the best job." He finished his coffee and placed his mug on the workbench. "Chelsea, are you sure you won't come and work with me? We'd have the best time."

"I'm sure," I said firmly, and for the umpteenth time. I'd go back to taking my clothes off and fucking men for money before I worked with him. Call me crazy, but I preferred sex to torture and killing. I suspected that, to him, they were all the same thing. Just another way to get off. To satisfy primal urges. Whatever did it for him, it didn't do it for me.

My intention was to scare Belinda, that was all, but once I'd done it, I knew I couldn't leave it at that. She would have called the police and I'd lose any chance I had of being team doctor to the Dusk Bay Smashers rugby union team. Not to mention being inconvenienced while my family worked to get me released from police custody.

What would Storm, Frost and Dallas say if they saw me here, like this? I'd like to think they'd be horrified, like any normal person. In reality, I suspected they'd like this side of me. The side that would shoot a woman's computer and bring her down here at gunpoint, knowing she wouldn't walk out of here again. The side that wouldn't give up on my dreams without a fight. Even a dirty fight.

When it came down to it, there was nothing I wouldn't do to get what I wanted. We all had that in common: me, my brother and my boyfriends. We were all ambitious. Driven to the point of ruthlessness.

"I'll keep working on you." He booped the tip of my nose with his finger before stepping over to open a drawer on the side of the room. "I can't decide if I'm in a toenail mood or a fingernail mood." He pulled a pair of pliers out of the drawer. "Some days, it's so hard to decide. Can I at least convince you to decide for me?" He gestured towards his 'guest' with the pliers.

"What are you doing?" Belinda took a step back as if there was anywhere to go, pulling the chains to their fullest extent.

"We're getting started," Ice said cheerfully. "I don't want to keep you hanging." He chuckled to himself.

I snorted. "Ba dum tish."

Being the smartass that he was, he actually bowed, making his dark ponytail swing to the side.

"See what you're missing?" He straightened back up and stepped over to Belinda. "You could have fun with people like this, and enjoy my sense of humour at the same time." He grabbed her hand and pulled it closer to his face. He gripped onto the fingernail of her pointer finger with the pliers and started to work it loose from its bed.

I winced and turned my face away, but I couldn't shut out the sound of her scream of pain. She would have destroyed my life, but this was still horrible to watch. As many times as I'd seen him work, I was nowhere near used to it. No matter how deserving the victim. He got off on this, but I didn't think I ever would.

"Kennedy used to have the same response," Ice said. "But now, she enjoys my work as much as I do."

I never saw his girlfriend down in his workroom, but I took his word for it. There was a darkness in her like there was in both of us. Apparently she was better at surrendering to hers than I was at surrendering to mine. Honestly though, I couldn't imagine anyone enjoying this as much as my brother did. He'd always been fascinated by people and the way they worked. Why some people felt more pain than others; how far he could push people to make them scream, beg or die.

When was the first time he killed another person? I didn't know. He probably remembered, like anyone remembers their first time doing something life changing. It wouldn't surprise me if he'd lost count since then. Ironically, he'd never hurt a kitten or a puppy. If he saw anyone abusing an animal, he'd likely strangle them with his bare hands. Lucky for him, because if he did anything to a small animal, he'd have to deal with me.

"I should get going." I glanced back in time to see him starting on the second nail. My breakfast threatened to come back up.

"No, please," Belinda begged. "I swear I'll do anything you want. Please." Her eyes bulged wide, more white than irises or pupils. Her face was just as white, like all the blood drained down to her nail bed, where it now dripped. The tang of urine filled the room. The puddle at her feet trickled into a drain beside the wall.

If Ice didn't clean his workroom thoroughly after each of his guests, it would mingle with the blood of countless other people who came before her. As it was, the concrete floor looked almost immaculate. My brother was nothing if not meticulous with maintaining the cleanliness of his space. Like any good doctor.

I eyed the gun lying on the workbench. I couldn't let her out of here, but I could end her suffering faster. One bullet right into her brain and she wouldn't feel a thing. She'd be dead and I'd never have to worry about her again. She wouldn't have to endure the pain my brother was going to put her through the next few days. The agony. The torture.

I picked up our empty mugs and carried them upstairs to be washed.

I was many things, but I wasn't a killer.

Chapter Two

Chelsea

"Oh, shit," Sadie whispered. "She was really going to do that to you?" She poured a generous glass of wine and handed it to me. "Why didn't you tell me this before you went to her place?"

I took the glass and lowered myself down onto the couch, one leg under me, careful not to spill any over the rim. "I didn't want to get you involved," I said with a sigh. "I was hoping to talk to her and convince her to back off. She wouldn't. She was going to publish that article, telling the world I used to work at Flirts, and that she saw me with the guys."

Sadie winced. "That would have gone down well with Smashers' management."

"Exactly." I downed a gulp of wine. "We both know what would have happened then. They would have made excuses for the guys, and I would have been burnt at the proverbial stake."

She sat beside me and leaned over to pat my knee. "I hate to say it, but that's exactly what would have happened. Guys like that always get out of things like this."

"That's why they have a PR department," I said, trying not to bristle. Was she suggesting they'd throw me under the bus and walk away without looking back?

"It seems to me like they don't need one," she said lightly. "You had the situation under control."

I relaxed against the back of the couch and exhaled slowly. Of course she wasn't pointing fingers, I was just on edge.

"Did I?" I rubbed my temples with my fingertips. "A simple conversation turned into getting my brother involved."

"From what I've seen of him, I'm sure he didn't mind," she assured me. "Belinda seemed, I don't know, unreasonable when I met her. I get the impression nothing short of what you actually did would have convinced her to drop it. Or killing her. She was so sure she was onto something that was going to make her a shit ton of money. That was all she cared about. She wasn't worried about your feelings. Or how your guys would think about any of this. But here you are, worried about what she's going through." Her expression softened on my behalf.

"I *am* a doctor," I said. "It's my job to help people, not put them through...whatever my brother is doing to her." Should I have put my pride aside and ended her life to save her from suffering? What would my brother have thought of that? I was almost certain he would have supported my decision, but at the same time, he might have been disappointed to miss out on a research opportunity.

Either way, I couldn't undo what I hadn't done.

"Regrets?" Sadie asked.

That was a good question and required some thought before I could give her an honest answer.

"No," I said finally. "What choice did I have? I had to do what I did, or sit back and watch my life implode. After which, my brother would have done what I did anyway, out of retribution. Either way, she would have ended up the same."

"Honestly, I need to find me a man who looks after me the way your brother looks after you," she said. "But one who fucks like your three rugby play-ers. How does it feel to have a blessed life?"

I snorted into my wine. "It doesn't feel very blessed right now. What happens when the next person finds out what I used to do? I might not be so lucky again. They might tell the whole world before I could get to them and stop them. Or I might have to do what I did tonight, again. How many times am I supposed to do that? Maybe I *should* go and work with my brother. Working for the team feels like a ticking time bomb."

"What kind of talk is that?" she scolded. "You're an amazing doctor and you've worked hard to get where you are. You used to take your clothes off for a living, so what? You don't deserve to be vilified for it." She regarded me for a moment. "This isn't about that, is it? This is guilt about handing that woman over to your brother. Even after all she would have done to you, you feel bad for doing it."

She knew me too well.

"I feel bad for *having* to do it," I said. "I could have offered her money. I could have given her the names of I-don't-know-how-many different men that frequented Flirts. Names that would have made her a lot more money than three rugby players, even high profile ones." Powerful men who would have done anything to keep the world from finding out what they got up to behind the doors of the club.

"She still would have published that article, and you know it," Sadie reasoned. "She would have taken those other names and happily pressed enter. She wouldn't have lost any sleep over it either. But you know what, if she published the names of any of those powerful people, she'd end up dead anyway."

Sadie tended bar at Flirts. She knew exactly who I was referring to. She also knew I wouldn't have told Belinda anything. My job at the club relied on discretion as much as my job as a doctor did. It was something I took seriously, no matter how desperate I was.

"When you play with fire, you get burnt," she concluded. "If she wasn't smart enough to figure that out, that's her problem. Not yours. You shouldn't be worrying about anything she's going through right now. Just be glad it's not you with a phone blowing up, and the world all up in your business."

"You're right," I conceded.

"Of course I am. I'm always right," she said with a smile. "That's why you tell me things. So I can be the voice of reason on the rare occasion you lose yours. But I'm still cranky with you for not telling me what you were doing. I would have liked to see the expression on her face when you walked into her apartment and aimed a gun at her." She pointed a finger gun in my direction.

"Next time, I'll capture it on bodycam," I said

dryly. "Would you like me to stream my brother's torture sessions so you can watch?"

"Actually..." she said slowly.

I grimaced at her. "I'm going to pretend I didn't make that suggestion. I'm definitely not going to suggest it to my brother." He'd totally be on board with doing that. To be fair though, he probably thought of it already and dismissed the idea. Those he worked for didn't really like leaving evidence lying around.

Sadie pouted playfully. "Spoilsport. Maybe he'd let me watch some time."

"I'll pose that suggestion to him," I said. "I'm sure he wouldn't mind an audience. He's always been good at sharing. Who knows, you might come up with some creative ideas he hadn't thought of."

"You must have had a very interesting childhood," she remarked. "With a big brother who likes to torture people, I bet no one got away with doing anything bad to you."

"They didn't, because I learnt to stand up for myself," I said.

Although, now she mentioned it, one of my high school teachers went missing under mysterious circumstances. I couldn't have been more than twelve or thirteen at the time. My brother was about seventeen. Was he the first? Honestly, I didn't want to know. That particular teacher had commented on my weight and I never saw them again. I decided I wouldn't think about it too hard.

"You're such a badass," Sadie said. "I wish you had another brother. If he was anything like you and Ice, I'd totally go there." Her smile was nothing short of dreamy.

"If I'd had another brother, he'd be all yours," I assured her. That was an easy promise to make, considering it was only the two of us. That was probably just as well, I didn't think the world could cope with two Isaac Millers. Or two of me, for that matter.

"What are you going to tell your boyfriends?" she asked. "They might wonder why Belinda suddenly disappeared."

"I can't tell them anything," I regretfully. Some day, I might have to be forthcoming about the dark nature of Dusk Bay, but not yet. "My brother arranged a communication with her employer to say she had a family emergency. After that, she'll quietly disappear for a while. He assured me it was all taken care of. She won't be a problem for anyone else again.

"The guys will be happy she's gone," I added. "If I hadn't dealt with her, they might have, and they can't afford to do anything that would jeopardise their careers."

"Like strangling the living shit out of a paparazzo," Sadie suggested.

"Exactly." I nodded. "That's the kind of thing a professional rugby player would get in a little bit of trouble for."

"Or a lot of trouble," she said.

"Or a shit ton," I agreed. They would have done it, though. Frost might have drugged her so the other two could drag her off somewhere. I tried not to, but the mental image of Storm placing her into a bath and holding her under the water until she drowned popped into my head. His handsome face, intense grey eyes full of fury as he watched the life fade out of her.

I already knew I was fucked up, so the way my clit throbbed at the thought didn't surprise me. It should have disgusted me more than it did, but the mental image was...well, hot.

So was the thought of Dallas fucking me from behind while we watched Storm kill her.

What would they have thought of what was going on in my brain right now? If they had any sense, they'd run for the hills. If I had any sense, I'd let them.

"You didn't just do it for you," Sadie said. "You went over there to deal with that woman to protect them as well. So they wouldn't have to deal with the potential publicity her article would have drummed up. Because you don't want people saying things about them."

"Of course I don't," I said. "Because what they do behind closed doors is no one else's business. Even if it didn't impact their career now, it would be a cloud over them for the rest of their lives. Or at least until they retire from playing footy. And because of what? Because they wanted to see me naked. Big fucking deal."

I sucked in a hard breath. "I get it, they're role models for children, but they can be that out in public. Private should stay private. No one needs to know what really goes on."

Outside of spending time at Flirts, they did all the usual community stuff, being the good guys for kids to look up to. For aspiring rugby players to copy. That was all the public needed to see. The salacious side was none of their business. It didn't matter how famous they were, they didn't owe their fans every little detail of their lives. They didn't need to know Daniel Frost drugged and fucked me. They didn't need to know I was waiting for Storm Keller to whisk me away to get rough with me. They didn't need to know Dallas Gregory could hardly keep his cock out of me when we were together. They didn't need to know if I got involved with any other players on the team. Only we needed to know.

"Anyone who's upset by that is jealous they didn't get to see you naked," Sadie assured me. She'd seen me like that plenty of times at the club. She'd seen me bent over the couches, or on my knees giving a client a blowjob. She'd seen so much it probably didn't register anymore. I was just Chelsea doing my job, nothing more. No big deal.

"I'll keep telling myself that," I assured her. I might need it for the next time someone like Belinda popped up. I'd have to be on my guard, because it wasn't an if. It was a when, and there was only so much space in my brother's workroom.

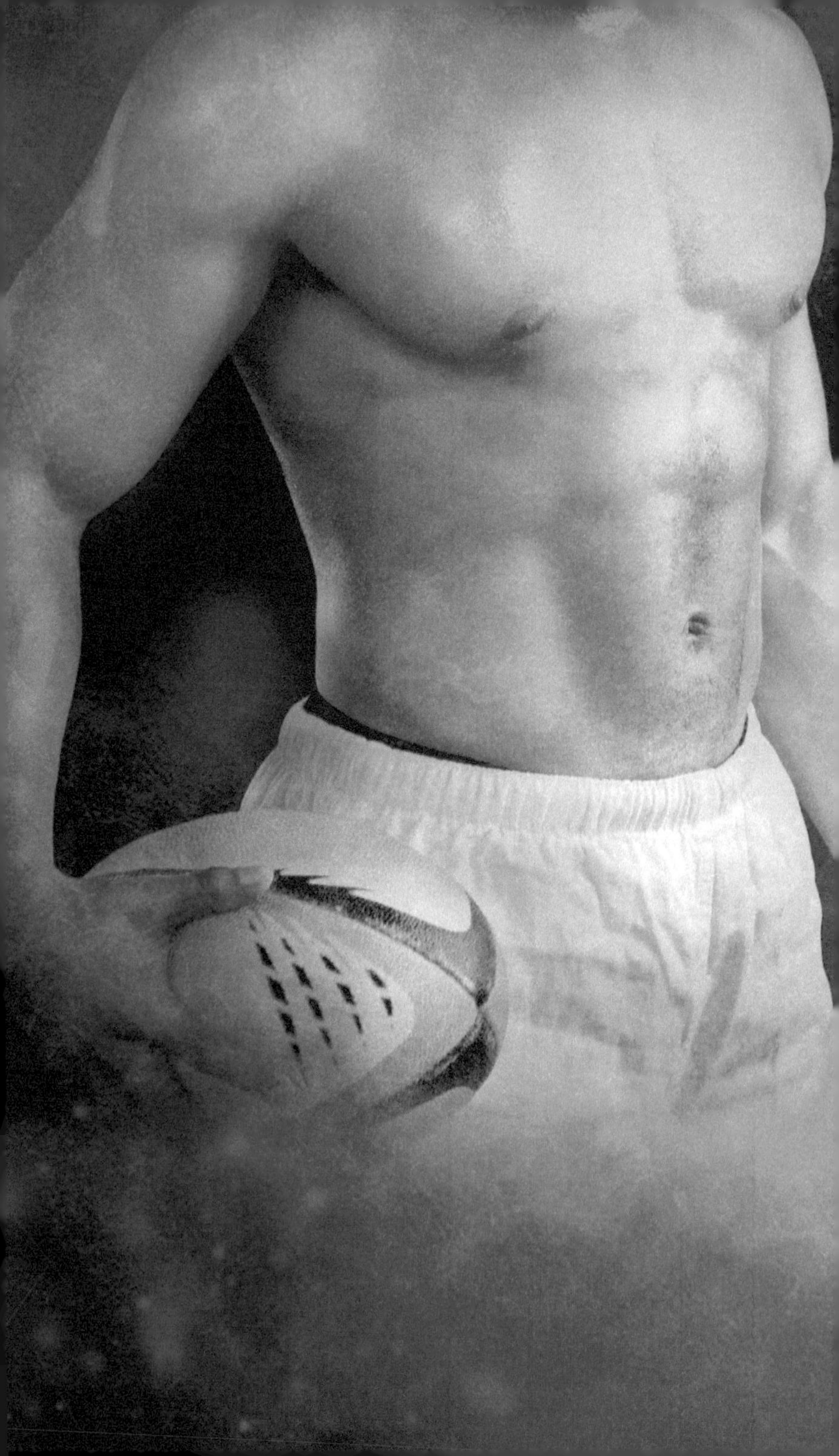

Chapter Three

Chelsea

I winced at the crunch of Storm's elbow slamming into Atlas' nose. From my position on the sidelines, it was painfully audible. And quickly followed by Atlas' shout of pain.

"Fucking hell!" He grabbed the hem of his jersey and pressed it to his nose to stem the gush of blood, while he trotted over to the edge of the field.

"I'll let you manage this," Doctor Stuart said as he nodded and stepped back. "Atlas, this is Doctor Chelsea Miller. She's fully qualified to take care of you."

Atlas gave me a sceptical look, which quickly changed to a speculative one. He glanced back over his shoulder at Storm, Frost and Dallas, who all glared in his direction.

For a moment, I thought they might try to stop me from treating him, but Coach called for them to focus and get back to training. They only hesitated for a moment before walking back into position, their backs to us. Each man held himself stiff, clearly still aware of what was going on behind him. Not liking it, but not having a choice either.

"We'll need to x-ray that," I said to Atlas. As a formality, because anyone could tell his nose was broken. Not for the first time, given the shape of it before this.

"Maybe it'll be even now," he said, his voice muffled with fabric and pain.

I smiled and walked beside him to the stadium's state-of-the-art infirmary. "I'll do what I can to make sure you stay pretty."

He snorted, then swore again. "Fuck. This is bullshit." He seemed to be more pissed off at himself for snorting than he was at the discomfort. No doubt he got used to the pain of injuries a long time ago.

I gestured for him to sit in a chair behind the x-ray machine and snapped on some gloves. When he lowered the front of his jersey, I wiped the blood away from his nose.

While I moved around, he followed me with his

light brown eyes. Almost gold, they were locked on my every movement.

"So you're Chelsea," he said.

"The one and only," I said lightly. I gave him an ice pack to press to his nose and walked over to the side of the infirmary to get a couple of painkillers and a cup of water.

More than my brother would have given anyone he was working on.

"You're a doctor," he stated. He threw back the pills and washed them down with water before handing back the cup.

"That's what it says on my degree," I said. "And you're Atlas Underwood, inside centre."

"Yep," he said. His gaze lingered on me again, like he expected me to say something else.

"I need you to lower the ice pack and sit still so we can see how broken it is," I said.

"Sure, Doc." Gingerly, he lowered the ice and half-closed his eyes, his body completely still.

I stepped back and let the x-ray technician do their job. While they took the images, I watched over their shoulder, glancing at the player every once in a while.

"Looks like a linear fracture," the tech said, only

loud enough for me to hear. "Not too bad, considering."

I squinted at the images on the screen. "I agree. It could have been worse."

"Why are you whispering?" Atlas snapped.

"We're conferring," I said easily. I waited for the technician to turn the machine off before stepping back around to the other side. "As we suspected, it's broken, but it's not too bad."

"Yeah, well, I didn't think it was life-threatening," he said, putting the ice back to his face.

"Not this time, no," I agreed. "You got lucky."

His golden eyes slid up and down my body. "Not yet I didn't."

"Keep the ice on your face for a while," I instructed. "We need to keep the swelling down as much as possible. It'll be that and ibuprofen for the next few days. How many times have you broken it before?" While we waited for his pain to ease, I turned on the computer and looked him up.

"Three times," he said. "The other two were by the opposition. Not a fucking so-called teammate." He all but spat out the last word.

"You and Storm don't get along," I said. I glanced over my shoulder at him before turning back and adding today's incident to his medical record.

"Storm is a dickhead," Atlas snapped. "His fucking friends too."

"Frost and Dallas," I said. I tried to keep my expression as neutral as possible. We weren't here to discuss my personal life. I certainly wasn't going to bring it into the conversation.

"Yeah, them. They all think they're king shit." He adjusted the ice and winced.

I turned and leaned my back against the wall beside the computer. I crossed my arms over my chest and asked, "What do you think?"

He tilted his face so I could see his smile. "I *know* I'm king shit. Me and Jay, we're too good for this fucking team. Everybody knows it and they're fucking jealous."

"You wish you were still back with the Sydney Devils," I guessed.

His gaze dropped to my chest for a few moments before returning to my face. "Wouldn't you? We won the premiership and got dumped into this shit hole. Wouldn't you be pissed off?"

"If I was team doctor for the Devils and had to transfer here, how would I feel?" I mused. "To be honest, I'd be happy just to be doing what I love."

He rolled his eyes and winced again. "Figures.

You're one of those glass half-full kind of people. The one who sees rainbows and puppies everywhere."

I lowered my hands to my sides and gave a short laugh. "Not at all. I just know when to appreciate what I have. The way I see it, you could either be miserable until you retire, or you can give the Smashers a kick in the ass to hand the Devils their asses on the field. What better revenge is there than beating them? Prove to your old team they made a mistake in letting you go. Personally, I'd pay to see the expressions on their faces. I bet you and Jay would too."

He looked sceptical, but my words gradually sank in, connecting to him, albeit grudgingly.

"I suppose," he grunted. "No reason why we can't beat them. We have me and Jay. Ramsey too, I guess."

I waited, head cocked with a hint of expectation.

"I guess the rest are okay players too, when they get their heads out of their asses," he conceded. "Kinda hard to play with guys who hate your guts."

"I don't know, but I have a feeling they'd say the same about you," I said, knowing full well that was exactly the case. We both knew it. No doubt both sides would blame the other. It was easier than accepting the blame yourself. That meant having to be the one to try to heal the rift between them. To be the bigger man. So to speak, since they were all big. The combined total of muscle on the team was impressive, to say the least.

"It seems to have eluded them exactly how awesome we are," he said. "Like I said, they all buried their heads."

"I have a funny feeling that's universal around here," I said. I wasn't going to pull any punches. I'd seen with my own eyes how the guys were with each other. Storm's elbow breaking Atlas' nose was an accident, but it could easily have been on purpose. Next time it might be, but I hoped not. That was the last thing the team needed. That and people like Belinda Simmons sniffing out the animosity and making a public deal out of it.

"This isn't where you say you think we should all be best buddies, is it?" He looked as though he'd prefer to have his pubic hairs pulled out one by one, with tweezers, than be friends with the other guys.

"Would it kill you?" I asked.

"One hundred percent," he shot back immediately. "You've met those guys. What the hell do you see in them anyway? You're fucking gorgeous and smart, you can do better than any of them." His tone was as scathing as the look in his eyes.

"Like you?" I asked teasingly.

He pushed himself to his feet and walked over to loom in front of me. Even at five-foot-ten, he made me feel small.

"Why not me?" he asked. "Unless those three have poisoned you against me." The look in his eyes was a challenge.

"I make up my own mind about people." I lifted my chin to stare him down. They didn't have anything nice to say about him, but that was their opinion. I could form my own conclusions, whether they liked it or not.

"I thought you might." Ice pack still firmly on his nose, he nodded slowly. "Go out with me. Make up your own mind. I bet you'll like what you see."

I had to admit I was intrigued. Partly *because* of what the other guys said, but mostly because of the man standing in front of me right now. He clearly had a big chip on his shoulder, but who wouldn't after losing a spot on the premiership winning team?

Yes, I'd be happy to be doing the job I loved, but at the same time I'd be hurt and angry. To go from the top, to a team that was less than welcoming, and feel like you had to work your way back up from the bottom? No wonder he was tense and frustrated.

"What are you proposing?" I asked. I was good at jumping in with both feet, but I wasn't going to do that now. This was a complicated situation that required careful footsteps, and open eyes. Otherwise, more than a nose might get broken.

"One date. No strings, no pressure. Just a good time. If you decide I'm the asshole the other guys think I am, I'll leave you alone. But you won't, I promise you that." His golden eyes were pure cocky. Atlas Underwood was used to getting what he wanted, that was abundantly clear. It was also clear that he'd like more than a date with me. Every so often, his gaze would drop, taking in my body under my blouse and pencil skirt. Appreciative.

"One date," I said. "You might decide I'm the asshole."

He groaned. "Don't make me laugh. I already know you're not an asshole. I'm a good judge of character."

Given he didn't like Storm, Frost or Dallas, I wasn't so sure he was right, but I didn't bother to correct him. That whole situation went deeper than character judgement. It was about wounded feelings of men who didn't like to admit they had emotions. It was about the pressure of being forced to come together as a team, when the circumstances weren't ideal.

Fortunately for them, they weren't part of my brother's lifestyle. If they were, someone would end up dead. Correction, they'd be dead already.

"I'll pick you up tonight after training," Atlas said. He held out his hand. "I'll give you my number so you can text me your address."

I pulled my phone out of my back pocket and handed it to him. Along with a side eye glance to suggest I thought he couldn't use it one-handed.

Like anyone with competitive blood running through their veins, he returned the look, held my phone in one hand and entered his number into the contacts with the other.

"You'll find me under 'Rugby God.'" He half closed one of his eyes before realising winking might hurt.

I bit back a smile and pressed my phone back in my pocket. "I'll text you later. I probably shouldn't do it at work." Especially since I was still a student. After I graduated, I could loosen up a little.

Although, I was already losing track of the amount of times Dallas and I fucked when Doctor

Stuart wasn't around. We were lucky no one had walked in on us.

So far.

Movement in the doorway caught my eye.

"What the fuck?" Frost asked.

Chapter Four

Frost

I DIDN'T GIVE A SHIT ABOUT ATLAS OR HIS broken nose. If I was honest, I actually headed to the infirmary after training to see how hard Chelsea kicked his ass. He was a sullen prick, even worse than Storm and Dallas. Not that I gave a shit, like I said. The guy was hot, but he was a stone cold asshole. If you ask me, he had the perfect name. He walked around like he had the weight of the world on his shoulders. Some people had to be too literal.

Not me though. My last name might be Frost, but I'm never cold with anyone, especially Chelsea and Storm. Let's be real here, if *I* lived up to my name I'd be an absolute prick.

Standing in the doorway, trying to wrap my head around what I just witnessed, I could easily be one.

If I didn't know better, I'd think Atlas gave Chelsea his number. With her knowledge and consent. What the fuck was he playing at?

A little voice in the back of my head asked, *What is she playing at?*

Atlas turned slowly, ice pack pressed against his annoyingly attractive face. "None of your fucking business."

I smirked and turned my attention to Chelsea. "I wasn't asking him, I was asking you. Why did he need your phone?" I was hoping she'd have some response that made sense. Something that wasn't what I thought I saw.

"He was giving me his number," she said easily.

"What for?" I asked. *Please tell me it's a medical situation.* If it wasn't, it might become one.

"He asked me out on a date," she replied in the same tone.

"You needed his number so you could tell him no?" I guessed. That had to be it, right? "You can tell him no right to his face." Without glancing at him, I gestured toward Atlas.

He was built about the same as me. In a fight, I'd have the advantage that he was already injured. Otherwise, we'd be relatively evenly matched.

"I've got a better idea," Atlas said. "It's called

'mind your own fucking business.' If the good doctor wants to go out with me, that's her choice. Right, Chelsea?"

I slowly turned and gave him half an eye. "Did I mention I wasn't asking you?"

"I don't know, I wasn't listening," he said. To Chelsea he said, "I look forward to your text. Thanks for the ice pack." He held it up, to toast her with it before shouldering past me and heading out into the corridor.

I pinched myself.

"Not dreaming. Why the hell would you want to go out with him?" In this case, being good-looking was no excuse. Neither was having a big cock. The chip on his shoulder was bigger.

"Why wouldn't I?" She pulled off a pair of rubber gloves and flicked them into the rubbish bin. "I'm not committed to anyone."

I have to admit, that stung. I was totally committed to her and to Storm. Not formally. We hadn't talked about it yet, but in my brain we were solid.

"I don't see it that way," I said.

"I thought you might not." She turned on a tap and started to wash her hands. "That whole, 'you guys own me,' thing."

"You didn't seem to have a problem with that before." I crossed my arms over my chest and leaned against the wall beside her. "Storm is going to be pissed."

She turned off the tap and grabbed a towel to dry her hands. "Storm is going to have to deal with it. We've already discussed the possibility of me seeing other men. Other men might include Atlas." She lifted her chin, all defiance, asking for her ass to be smacked in punishment.

I ran a hand through my hair, which was still damp from the thirty second shower I'd basically run through. "What does this mean?"

She tossed the towel in the rubbish bin, turned to face me and crossed her own arms.

"Why does it have to mean anything? I have three holes and two hands. Not to mention, at some point, you and Storm are going to give in to the attraction between you. I don't see any harm in exploring every possibility that comes our way."

She had a point. Storm and I had kissed and I liked it. I knew she liked watching. I wanted more, but I wasn't going to push him, not yet. At some point though, yes, we would fuck each other.

But Atlas Underwood? In spite of being hot, he wasn't on the list of possible candidates to share

Chelsea with. Correction, he wasn't on *my* list. He seemed to very much be on hers.

"I mean, what if you like him more than us?" I asked. I hated to sound vulnerable. I was more in touch with that side of me than Storm or Dallas put together, but I was still supposed to be a big, badass rugby player. Not someone who'd lose their shit if they were looked at the wrong way.

Like Atlas.

She smiled softly and placed her hand on my cheek. "How could I possibly like him more than you?"

"I was wondering the exact same thing," I said. "I'm pretty awesome."

"Yes, you are." She moved her hand down to my shoulder and leaned over to kiss my cheek. "You're very awesome."

"But you're still going on a date with him." I grabbed her wrist to keep her close.

"Yes, I am," she said, her eyes on my hand. "You have to know I wouldn't have done it without telling you guys first. I have no intention of going behind anyone's back. Whatever we have building here, it won't work without communication."

"Which brings me back to going out with Atlas,"

I said. "His idea of communication is a middle finger and telling people to fuck off."

She laughed softly. "He seemed a lot nicer than that to me. Maybe you should give him a chance."

I grimaced. "That was what Dallas said. That we should lay off and give him a break." He was new to the team and still finding his feet, but he didn't have to do that and be an asshole at the same time.

"Apparently Dallas is wiser than I thought," she said.

"He hides it well," I agreed. When it came to Chelsea, Dallas had a difficult time communicating with words. Mostly, he communicated with thrusts. Of his cock. Into her body. The man couldn't get enough of her. It was a minor miracle he wasn't here right now, getting a hit of her presence. No doubt he'd rectify that soon enough.

"Maybe I should make it a group date," she mused, a smile tugging at the corners of her lips. "The three of you, me and him. We could throw in Jay and Ramsey for good measure."

"The numbers would be even when the fists started flying," I said with a grimace.

No doubt they would. Storm couldn't be in the same room as Atlas and Jay without starting something.

Ramsey would shake his head and slink away, probably to the gym. He was a man of few words, but lots of judgement. A man who tended to take Atlas and Jay's side. Why? You'd have to ask him. Even if I asked him directly, I doubted he'd give me an answer.

She laughed. "Let's put that in the maybe pile then. I don't think the team would be happy with me if you all turned up the next day battered and bruised. You get enough of that on the field without doing it to each other in your spare time."

"Nothing we couldn't handle," I said, not bothering to contain the bragging tone that always came with declarations like that. "But you'd have to slip Storm something before he'd turn up for anything with them."

I tangled my fingers in her dark hair and thought back to our date together. She let me slip a sedative into her drink, and she drank it all. Every drop. I waited and watched while it started to work, until she was just this side of unconscious.

I carried her out to my car and placed her in the back seat. All she'd been able to do was watch me with those big blue eyes while I stripped her and fucked her. She'd been completely helpless, unable to stop me from doing everything I wanted to her.

She let me do all of it. She was as into it as I was.

She wanted to let me live out my wildest fantasy with her; being in complete control of her.

Storm, being the protective prick he is, found us right after I came inside her, and assumed I forced myself on her. Until he knew what really happened, that was. Now, he was down for us doing it to her, again. He and I, together. My pulse ratcheted up in anticipation. More so at the idea of him letting me do the same to him. Having them both completely powerless in front of me was the ultimate fantasy. Would he go for that? I wasn't sure, but I wouldn't stop hoping.

"That's actually tempting," she said.

I blinked, trying to remember what we were talking about. My mind was lost in the past for a while and my cock was now hard. Right, drugging Storm.

"Not without his permission," I said. Not that I thought for a moment she'd do it otherwise. Even if she wasn't a doctor, she respected consent as much as we did. Our fantasies might be considered wild to some, but they'd only happen if everyone was on board. Completely understanding what they were consenting to, and outlining hard limits in return. It involved a shit ton of trust, but it was more than worth it. The other night was ironclad proof of that.

"Agreed, but if he doesn't at least make an effort to be tolerant towards Atlas, I might reconsider," she said dryly.

"As long as you don't do it without me there," I said.

If anyone was going to drug my best friend, I wanted to be present. Although, I'd make myself scarce when he recovered. Storm would definitely come back swinging. And he wouldn't care who his fist connected with. Unless it was Chelsea. Then it would be his hand on her ass. Hard enough to leave a handprint for a week.

"I'll try to include you," she said, teasing.

My hand still on her wrist, I pulled her until she was pressed against my chest. "Don't just *try*, woman," I growled.

"What are you going to do?" She looked me square in the eyes, blue eyes defiant.

"I'd make you suck my cock until you gag," I said. "And then I'd make you take me in even deeper. I'd fuck your mouth so hard you wouldn't be able to talk for a week."

"Daniel Frost." She clicked her tongue. "What have I said about threatening me with a good time?"

I lifted one eyebrow. "Come with me." My hand around hers, I pulled her out of the room towards the nearest toilet. Being for staff, it was unisex, not that I cared. My mind was on one thing.

I pushed her through the doorway in front of me, before closing and locking the door behind us.

My hand on her shoulder, I pushed her down to her knees and shoved down the front of my track pants and boxers. My erection sprang free, pointing straight at her.

"Open your mouth," I said, doing my best impression of Storm. I pressed the head of my cock against her lips until she opened her mouth. My head and a good portion of my length disappeared inside.

I tangled my hand in her hair and started to thrust between her lips pushing in deep until she gagged on me.

"Look at me," I said.

She tipped her chin back, her gaze on me while I fucked her mouth hard. Every time I slid all the way in, she gagged, but made no attempt to pull back.

I thrust into her with relentless, even strokes until my balls tightened almost to the point of pain. My eyes on her face, I let myself go, exploding inside her. My release gushed to the back of her mouth, forcing her to swallow before she drowned on my cum.

"Was that a good time?" I asked, still trying to catch my breath.

She made a sound of confirmation in the back of her throat and let her eyes smile.

"Of course it was," I said. This woman was fucking everything.

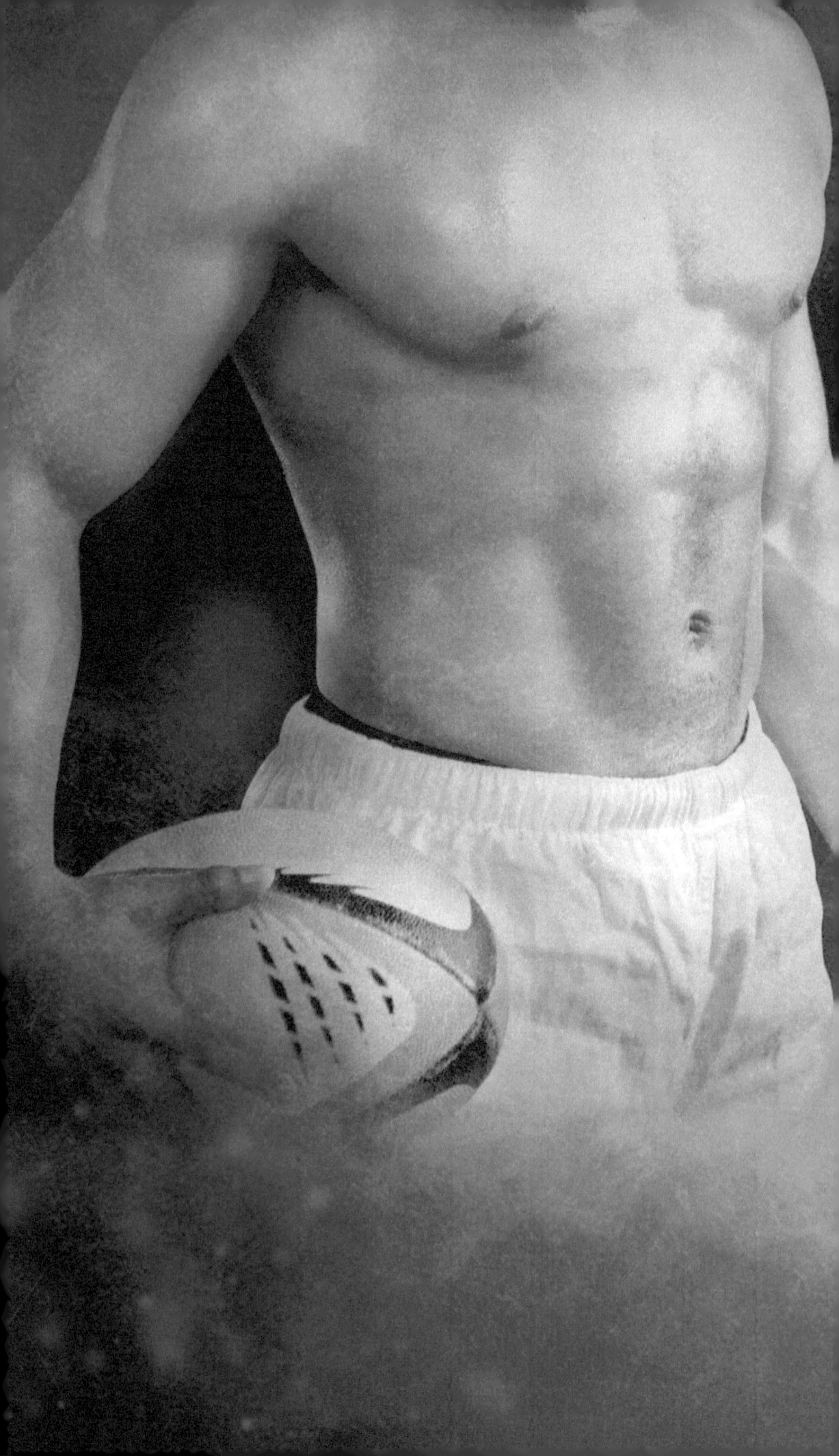

Chapter Five

Chelsea

"Are you sure about this?" I slid into the passenger seat of Atlas' truck and clicked my seatbelt into place. "I don't want the other guys making trouble for you." I'd told them exactly what was going on tonight. They weren't happy, but I'd made it as clear to Storm and Dallas as I had to Frost. The choice was mine. At some point, that might bite me in the ass, but I was going to enjoy the evening, and Atlas' company. In the end, it was Frost who insisted they let me go. With a silent promise of more good times.

Atlas clicked his own seatbelt and started the engine. "Nothing I can't handle. Those pricks can't dish out any shit I haven't seen before." He glanced over and gave me a grin that did things to my pulse rate. His face was still bruised, which only added to his charm. Being attractive must be a requirement for playing for the Smashers.

He pushed a few stray curls off his forehead and turned his attention to navigating the streets of Dusk Bay.

"I can't decide if you're saying they're unoriginal or if people have been shitty to you in the past," I said after a couple of minutes of silence.

He didn't respond for a moment. When he did, he said, "Both." He accompanied the word with a small shrug. "It comes with the territory. Old team, new team, whatever."

"You didn't get along with your former teammates?" Until now, it hadn't occurred to me that might be the case.

"Only Jay," he said. Again with a shrug. "I'm not the easiest person to get along with."

"You seem nice enough to me," I said.

"Tell you a secret?" he said.

"Of course." If he wanted to trust me with anything, no one would hear it from me. Fuck knows I had plenty of my own. Leaving a woman hanging by chains in my brother's workroom was only the most recent.

"I'm the youngest of six," he said. "The only boy.

Dad left when I was two. Since then, I get along with women better than men."

"How many times did they dress you up as a fairy princess?" I asked.

He ended a longer silence with the words, "Too many."

"So you took up football." One of the most brutal sports a person could play.

He let out a frustrated sigh. "Two of my sisters played. They got me into it."

"That's kinda sweet," I said.

He glanced over at me and grimaced. "Yeah, exactly. Assholes on my team used to call me Princess Atlas. I got them back by punching them in the face."

"How old were you?" I asked.

"About eight. Don't know how I didn't get kicked off the team."

Now I was picturing eight-year-old Atlas, a head full of curls, running around the footy field, taking swings at the other kids.

"I bet you were a handful," I said.

He glanced over again and grinned. "Babe, I've always been a handful."

I glanced down at his groin. "I'm sure you are." He certainly looked like it.

"Happy to show you any time." He pulled the truck onto the highway and drove for a few more minutes before pulling into a parking lot beside a small deserted beach.

"Isn't this private property?" I glanced around before I followed him out of the truck.

"Yep." He opened the back of the truck and pulled out a blue, plastic cooler. As long as his arm and almost as wide, it looked heavy. He made it seem effortless as he carried it to the beach, only the bulging of his biceps giving away the effort.

He lowered the cooler to the sand beside an unlit fire. He opened it, grabbed out a blanket and flicked it open.

He gestured for me to sit, before crouching beside the fire to get it started with a gas lighter. In moments, he had flames dancing, warming the cool evening.

"Let me guess, you own the place," I said.

He glanced over at me as he tossed the lighter back into the cooler. "Yep. The beach and the ten acres around us." He snatched up a couple of sticks that lay in the sand and took sausages out of the cooler. He speared the sticks through the centre of each sausage and handed one to me.

"I've never been big on fancy restaurants. Too

many people watching you, curious about what you're doing." He sat beside me and dangled his sausage amongst the flames.

I followed his lead, watching carefully so I didn't burn mine.

"I've noticed that," I said. Had he had run-ins with Belinda? Chances were, he had. People like her got around. Until they didn't. "Any regrets about going pro?"

"Only that one. Being scrutinised sucks." He turned his sausage to cook the other side. "And having to put up with dickheads like Storm Keller." He glanced back in the direction of the road, as if expecting the fullback to appear and try to whisk me away.

"Storm isn't so bad." I turned my own sausage. "But this is nice." The fire was warm enough to fend off the rapidly cooling air. The flames reflected off the waves, making them dance as they rolled onto the sand.

"I don't usually bring people here," Atlas said quietly. "I wanted us to go where we wouldn't be disturbed. By anyone."

"Are you talking about paparazzi, your team-mates or both?" I asked, although I knew the answer. I got the impression he hadn't had many male friends growing up. Like there were things girls only talked to other girls about, there must have been things boys kept between themselves. Not having that must have been difficult.

"Both," he agreed. "Are they going to give you shit about going out with me?"

I responded the way he had. "Nothing I can't handle. I'm seeing all three of them, but we're not exclusive."

"But you will be." He pulled his sausage out of the flames, inspected it before plunging it back in.

"I might be," I said. "Not with only one of them."

He looked at me in surprise and almost dropped his stick. He grabbed it at the last moment and turned his sausage around. "You're planning on having a long-term relationship with more than one of them?"

"Have you seen them?" I asked, joking lightly. "How could I choose one?"

"No idea," he said dryly. "I don't know how you could choose *any* of them."

"You want me to choose you?" I kept the same joking tone, but I was curious. We hardly knew each other, but he was willing to insert himself into an already complicated situation. Most guys wouldn't.

There was definitely more to the inside centre than I previously suspected.

"If I was you, I'd choose me," he said evasively. "What happens if you want me and them?"

"Then you have to learn to get along with each other," I said bluntly. "I'm a lover, not a mediator." I decided my sausage was cooked and pulled it out of the fire. It was perfectly black on the outside. The smell made my mouth water.

Atlas handed me a couple of slices of bread and a bottle of tomato sauce. I squeezed on a big dollop before handing the bottle back to him and taking a bite.

"Mmm, so good." The fire gave the meat a smoky flavour that only made it more delicious.

Atlas bit into his and nodded. "Nothing like food cooked on a fire." Holding his in one hand, he reached into the cooler for a couple of beers. He opened both with his teeth and spat the lids aside, before handing one to me.

"Lucky I'm your doctor, not your dentist." I nodded my thanks and swallowed down a gulp.

"Is that your goal?" he asked. "Team doctor for the Smashers?"

"Yeah, it is," I said. There was no point in not answering honestly.

"Why them... Us?" he quickly corrected. "Why not the Devils? Or any other team? Why rugby?"

"Dusk Bay is my home," I said. "And I might be obsessed with rugby players... I mean, rugby." I grinned before taking another bite of my sausage.

"I think you meant the first one," he teased. His expression quickly turned intense. His moods seem to change like the flick of a switch. Light one moment, dark and brooding in the next. If he wasn't careful, he'd give me whiplash. "What do I have to do to make you obsessed with me?"

"Do you have marshmallows in that cooler?" I peered over but couldn't see inside.

"If marshmallows are all it'll take, I'll buy you a truck full." Flames flickered in his golden eyes. His mischievous side was back, for now.

"I don't need a truck full," I said. "It'll take more than marshmallows to impress me anyway. They'd be a good start, though." I didn't mind surrendering to my sweet tooth once in a while. Especially if it took my mind off Belinda, wondering if she was still alive. If she hadn't harassed me and the guys, she might have enjoyed toasting marshmallows on the beach with someone. There was no doubt in my mind she was regretting that life choice, if she was still breathing. If she wasn't, I didn't want to know what my brother did with her. The less I knew, the better. As long as he kept me out of it. No one would ever know I was involved.

"Only a Neanderthal or an idiot would take a woman to a beach with a fire and not bring marshmallows," Atlas said. "Of course I brought those."

Before I could say anything else, he added, "Growing up with five women, they made sure I wasn't oblivious. I just give the impression I'm a massive meathead."

"There's definitely more to you than meets the eye, Atlas Underwood. You have me intrigued." I meant that. His switches of mood and seeing the real him after what the guys said, were fascinating. I suspected there was a good guy under the tough exterior.

"You have me intrigued too, Doctor Chelsea Miller," he told me. "Did you always want to be a doctor?"

"More or less," I said. "Once I realised I wasn't going to make it as a rugby player myself. Or a soccer player. Or a swimmer. The only things I was ever good at were dancing, and healing people." I looked over at him.

"Is that what you're doing?" he asked softly. "Healing me?" If he knew about the kind of dancing

I used to do, he gave no indication. Either he didn't know, or he knew and didn't care. I suspected it was the former. Most guys couldn't help themselves when they knew I took my clothes off for money. He might be that restrained, but I suspected not.

"I don't think you're as broken as you think you are," I told him.

"No?" He looked sceptical. "I could be more broken than I think I am. Which is only slightly less broken than Storm Keller."

"I think he'd consider that a compliment," I remarked. Storm seemed to get off on his own brokenness. Revelled in it. He claimed he owned me and never backed down from that. Never had a moment of indecision or regret. He didn't care how fucked up it was. I was his, that was that.

Atlas snorted just as he was about to take a sip of beer, making the bottle whistle. "Not even a little bit surprised. He likes being an asshole. The second he knew the Smashers signed me and Jay, he decided to make life hell for us. He can't fucking help himself."

"What about you?" I asked bluntly. "Did you take your frustration at the transfer out on him and the other guys?"

"Yep," Atlas said with no hesitation. "I did, and

so did Jay. I wasn't going to pretend I was fucking happy about it. I'm not."

"If the Devils were able to take you back, would you go?" I asked.

Now he hesitated. "A week ago, I wouldn't have answered that. I would have been too busy packing already. Now..."

"What's changed?" I asked.

"I met you," he said.

Chapter Six

Chelsea

THE MOMENT I CLIMBED OUT OF ATLAS' TRUCK, I knew I wasn't alone.

For a moment, I thought Belinda, or someone like her, was following me again. Or maybe my brother was lurking in the shadows, waiting to give me an update on her. He did that from time to time, for shits and giggles. Usually not to me though. Evidentially, I was on edge more than normal, after my run-ins with Belinda.

I turned on the light, held my phone in one hand and shone it around. "Who's there?" My voice sounded more confident than I felt, thankfully.

Something moved in the shadows.

No, some*one*.

Someone big.

They lunged toward me. Firm hands grabbed me and pushed dark fabric down over my head, over my face. They held it in place, clamping their hand over my mouth before I could make a sound.

I breathed in and out of my nose rapidly until I forced myself to a short-lived calm. Excitement ramped up and I smiled against the fabric and their large palm.

Someone else, there were at least two of them, pulled my arms behind my back and bound my wrists with narrow, hard plastic, tight enough that I couldn't pull my hands out. A cable tie.

My feet left the ground as I was lifted and carried a short distance. Without a word, I was bundled into a cramped, carpeted space, my knees bent before the boot was closed, locking me in.

I struggled and kicked, my sneakered shoes thudding against the inside of the car. As I expected, it didn't budge. A low chuckle preceded the closing of the car's other doors. Two distinct clunks.

The car started moving, rumbling underneath me as we headed away from my apartment building.

Surrendering to darkness compounded by what felt like a pillowcase over my head, I lay still again. All I could do now was wait. And overthink, but I couldn't help that. My brain was hardwired to do that, especially under circumstances like this.

I inhaled slowly. The pillowcase masked a hint of petrol or oil. The pillowcase itself smelled familiar. I made a face to myself. It smelled like one of mine. Like they'd broken into my apartment, went through my things and found this to put over my head.

I couldn't decide if that was thoughtful or disturbing. Probably a bit of both. So—normal in the life of Doctor Chelsea Miller. As normal as things ever got, that was.

Sadie, I thought quickly. Was she working that night? Yes, she was. She wouldn't have been home when they were there. That was a small mercy. She would have let them in if they explained why. At best, things might be awkward when I saw her next. At worst, she'd tease the hell out of me. Before asking if they had any single friends they could hook her up with.

I shook my head and tried not to hit the side of the boot as we took a corner too fast. If I had to bet, I'd suggest Storm was driving. The speed and rapid turns were threatening to make me nauseous.

Thank fuck, it didn't come to that. Before I lost my sausages and marshmallows, the road under the tyres turned to gravel. After another couple of minutes, the car slowed, then finally stopped.

The front door was opened and closed before footsteps walked around to the back of the vehicle.

The boot popped open. I tensed, waiting, ready to fight. Ready to make this as hard on them as possible. Pun absolutely intended.

Rough hands grabbed me and pulled me out of the back of the car. I writhed and struggled, but I was held firm against two hard bodies.

I heard the sound of a door opening, and footsteps walking down wooden stairs. A third set of hands grabbed my feet and I was carried upwards before the door closed behind us.

They carried me inside and tossed me down onto something soft. A mattress. I bounced once before lying still on what felt like the middle.

The moment I landed, I twisted, trying to crawl away.

Strong fingers grabbed my ankles and dragged me back, sliding me over cool sheets before flipping me onto my back.

Hands fumbled with the button of my jeans before working it loose and sliding down the zipper.

I struggled again, trying to pull away, but they

grabbed the sides of my jeans and held me in place before tugging them down.

Another pair of hands tore my panties away.

"Fucking hell," a familiar male voice said softly.

The adrenaline that rushed through my system made me kick out and try to work my hands out of the cable tie. I tried to hold my thighs together, but they were pushed apart and one of my kidnappers knelt between them. I tried to force them closed, but large hands grabbed my ass, raising me and impaling me on their thick cock.

I cried out with genuine pain that quickly faded.

A hand grabbed the top of the pillowcase, tugging my hair before it was yanked off and tossed aside. I expected to see three familiar faces, but they were covered with dark masks. One with black, one blood red and the other dark blue. They all watched me through the small slits made for their eyes.

All three men were naked, except for those masks. Rippling muscles on display, all carved, tattooed stone.

I couldn't remember a time when I'd been more turned on than I was right then, lying half-naked in front of three masked kidnappers. Heat pounded through my veins. I was drenched, my wet heat wrapped around an engorged cock.

Stormy grey eyes looked down into mine as he thrust into my slick pussy.

Green eyes, slightly less intense, sat beside me on the mattress, avidly watching me being fucked.

Hazel eyes, that bordered on manic, knelt and turned my face toward him, pressing his cock between my lips.

I tried to pull my face away, but he held my chin in a grip tight enough to bruise. He pushed into my mouth, deep enough to make me gag.

Green Eyes reached over to grab my hair, holding me in place so Hazel Eyes could fuck my mouth.

Gagging repeatedly brought tears to my eyes that soon trickled down my cheeks. My mascara was ruined by now. I was more than here for it. I'd never been down for anything more in my life.

On some signal I couldn't see, Stormy Grey Eyes rolled us over so I was on top of him, straddling his hips, impaled on his cock.

Green Eyes released my hair and grabbed lube to smear over my rear hole. It was cold enough to make me shiver, but I was so hot, I welcomed it.

Green Eyes pushed me forward and straddled Grey Eye's legs before slowly pushing his cock into my ass.

Once again, I tried to struggle, moving my ass to the side, trying to stop him from thrusting in any further.

He slapped my ass, hard enough to sting. "Bad girl."

His words sent another pulse of blood to my pussy. That's what I was. Their bad girl. The one they needed to punish, to force, to bend to their wills.

All three of them held me in place while I was impaled on two cocks. The third was forced back into my mouth.

I found myself being fucked relentlessly by all three of them. Hard, demanding, ruthless. They held back nothing, bringing me to the point of pain and beyond and never slowing.

I came so hard I saw stars in at least a dozen distant universes. I arched my back and screamed around my mouthful of hot cock. Bliss went on and on, maybe for minutes, maybe for days before starting to fade. It took the edge off, but I wasn't done yet. Just for the moment.

I was still catching my breath when Hazel Eyes came, squirting cum down the back of my throat, making me gag again. He held his cock there until I swallowed every salty drop.

"Fuck." His orgasm was quickly followed by Grey Eyes, and then Green. Grinding, and grunting, thrusting in unison until I felt like they might tear me apart.

Finally, they stilled, filling my pussy and my ass with their release.

Almost as one, they sagged, panting for a few moments before they slowly, carefully, slipped out of my stinging body. They lowered me back to the mattress.

Grey Eyes reached to the side of the bed for something, coming back with a knife. He rolled me over and sliced off the cable tie, but then nodded for the other two to fasten my hands to handcuffs attached to the bed.

"You made me angry," Grey Eyes said. The first time he'd spoken since they took me. "I told you, you belong to me. You dared to go out with another man."

I lifted my chin in defiance. Every bit their bad girl. "You knew about it."

He pressed the knife to my neck, just enough to draw a drop of blood. "Knowing about it doesn't make me less pissed off. Did you fuck him?"

I didn't answer.

He pressed the knife in slightly deeper, the edge of pain making my pussy throb again.

"Did. You. Fuck. Him?"

"Not yet," I said, breathless with the sudden increase in need.

Blood trickled down my neck. A normal person would have been scared, but I wanted more.

He switched to another spot on my neck and pressed down again. "You're going to."

"I want to," I said.

More blood trickled. With each nick, my clit throbbed harder. Aching for my own release.

"Be careful," Green Eyes said. "You might—"

"I know what I'm doing," Grey Eyes snapped. To prove a point, he pressed in again.

I moaned softly. Everything about this was arousing as hell. I had no control, but I had all of the control. The perfect balance of give and take. I was sticky with my own blood and their cum.

I *needed* more. Much more.

Grey Eyes leaned in, until we were almost nose to nose. The fabric of his mask brushed my cheek. "Who owns you?"

I knew the answer he wanted, but I responded with, "I own myself."

He moved the knife to another spot and sliced in lightly. "Who. Owns. You?"

I quivered with need. If he kept doing that, I'd come without anyone touching my pussy. "I own myself."

He growled, tossed the knife aside and rolled me over onto my stomach. He slapped his hand down on my ass hard enough to make me cry out. Again and again until my cheeks must have been flaming red.

I lost count of how many times he slapped me before he forced my legs open and dove down between them with his face. He rubbed his mask against my pussy. Against my clit. The friction from the fabric and his face behind it made me buck against him, grinding until I was on the verge of orgasm.

At the last moment, he pulled away, flipped me over and thrust a couple of fingers deep into my pussy. He curled his fingers inside me, almost clawing at me while the heel of his hand rubbed over my clit, rough skin scraping against the sensitivity.

Hazel Eyes grabbed the front of my blouse and tore it open, making buttons fly. He yanked the top of my bra down and bit his teeth into my nipple. The fabric of his mask doing nothing to blunt his teeth.

I arched my back and screamed in pain. It felt incredible. He must have seen that on my face, because he bit the other one. I screamed again, but then I was coming, crying out with a combination of bliss and pain.

I ground myself against the black mask, drawing out my orgasm for at least a minute. Everything disappeared but pleasure and rough hands and mouths.

I'd only begun to come down when Hazel Eyes was shoving Grey's hand out of the way and turning me toward him. He lifted my hips and rammed inside me.

I cried out. I was already sore, but I didn't try to pull away this time. He needed this and so did I.

"He's insatiable," Green Eyes said in awe. He pulled a key from the top of the headboard and unlocked the handcuffs, finally freeing my chafed wrists.

Grey Eyes grunted his agreement. Then he was grabbing Green Eyes' hand and pulling it down to his own cock, sticky with my release and his.

After a second of hesitation, Green Eyes wrapped his hand around it and started to pump.

"Your cock is so big," Green Eyes marvelled.

With his other hand, he massaged Grey Eyes' balls, all of his attention on the other man.

Hazel Eyes slowed his thrusts, taking his time to move inside me, even as his groans quickly grew to match mine. His cock was so thick he hit me all the way inside, driving me right back to the edge of oblivion.

Storm was the first to pull off his mask, dropping it aside right before he came in Frost's hand.

Frost was the second, removing his red mask with one hand before raising the other to his lips and licking Storm's cum from his skin.

The sight made me come for a third time, harder than the first two, stars in my eyes as I shattered around Dallas' cock.

With a low, guttural growl, Dallas came deep inside me, not taking off his own mask until he was done.

Finally, he lay down carefully, keeping himself inside me, but wrapped around me at the same time. He exhaled a satisfied sigh. Satisfied for now. If he could keep his cock inside my pussy for the rest of our lives, he would. That might be the only thing he'd give up football for.

To be honest, if it was possible, I'd be tempted to

give up medicine for this. His cock was perfect right there inside me.

"That was fucking amazing," Frost said. He lay down on the other side of Storm, propped up on one elbow.

"Everything I imagined," Storm whispered. "But we need to talk about Atlas."

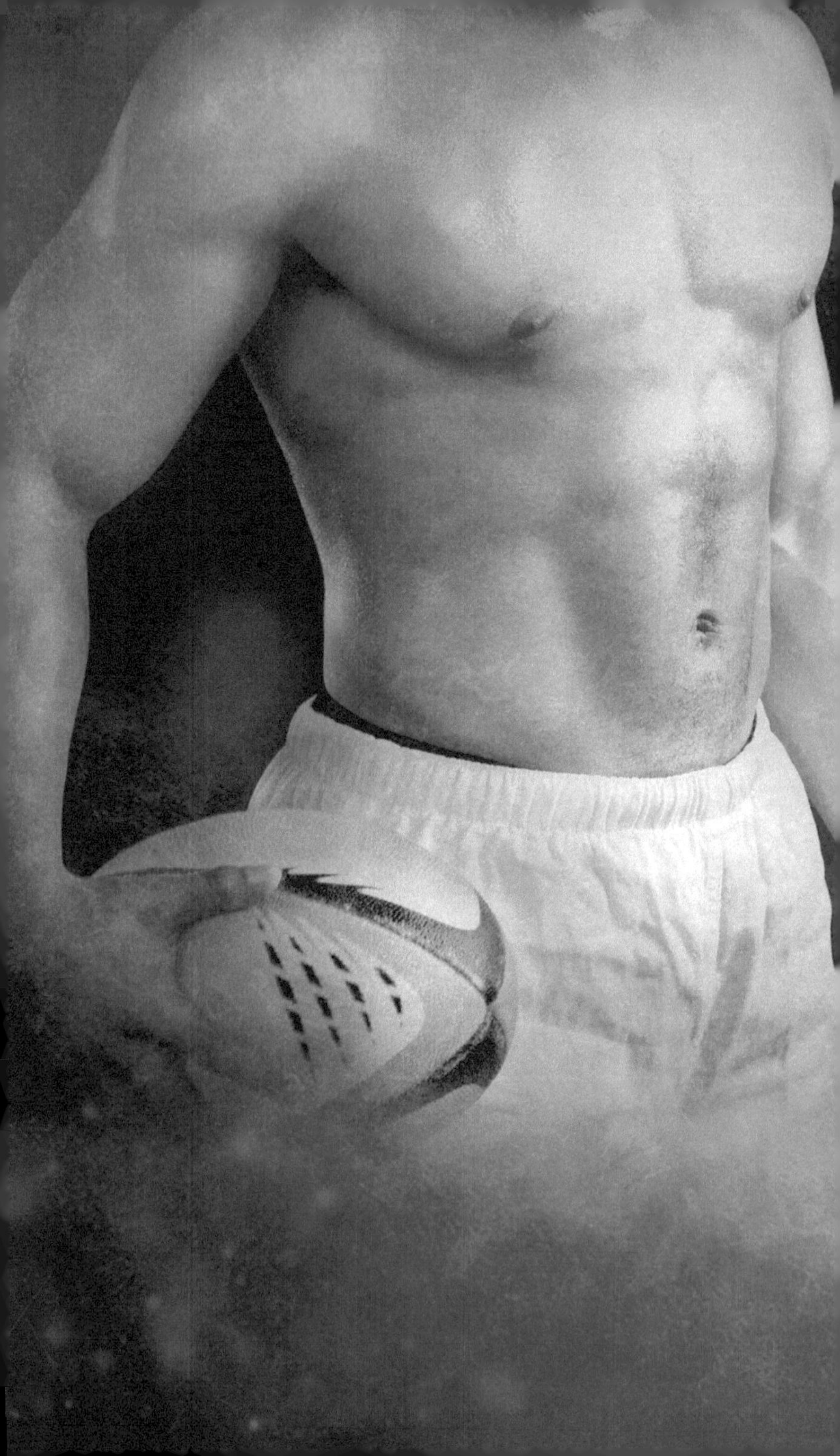

Chapter Seven

Frost

"I *told* you if Atlas saw her, he'd be into her," I whispered. I lay on the bed beside Storm, legs stretched out the full length of the mattress.

Dallas and Chelsea lay on the other side of Storm. Right now, they were fast asleep, both snoring lightly. He'd already fucked her twice more, but his cock was still inside her. If he wasn't careful, it would look like a prune from all the moisture.

Storm glanced over his shoulder to make sure they were still asleep, before turning back and pressing his lips together. "Yeah, but it's too late now. If she wants him, we'll have to deal."

I matched his expression. I suggested we try to get her as far away from the Smashers as possible. Between us, we hadn't managed to come to any conclusions that didn't involve pissing her off. And now, Atlas knew she existed.

I admit to being conflicted. Did I want to share her with more guys? Not really. But I wanted her to be happy, and if Atlas was here, I wouldn't kick him out of bed.

Personally, I suspected he and Jay had a thing going on, but they kept it from everyone else. Probably from themselves too. That hinted at a world of interesting possibilities. If that was what everyone wanted, I'd be crazy if I wasn't here for it, wouldn't I?

And yet, it wasn't that simple. Not by any means.

"How?" I asked. "In case you hadn't noticed, Atlas has never been too fond of either of us. We can't just walk up and say 'Hey, welcome to the family. Let's get matching jackets that say *Chelsea's boyfriends squad.* Or matching tattoos.'"

Storm snorted. "Fuck no. We should have our names tattooed on her. Right on her ass, so I can see it when I spank her."

"I have a better idea," I said. I cleared my throat before affecting a grand tone. "She can get *Property of Daniel Frost* tattooed on the inside of her thigh. Right where you can all see it when you spread her legs."

"And *Property of Storm Keller* on the other side,"

he said. He placed the pad of his thumb on the side of my face and traced a line down to the corner of my mouth. "And the same thing on you."

My heart thumped a couple of times. "You think so?"

"I know so." He pressed his thumb between my lips, letting me taste the salt on his skin. When I opened my mouth a little wider, he pushed it inside before I clamped my lips around and started to suck.

His eyes darkened. I knew we were both thinking the same thing. Pretending his thumb was his cock.

I slipped my mouth off him. "Storm..."

"Yeah?" Of course he wouldn't make this easy. The word probably wasn't in his vocabulary.

"I feel... Things," I said. "Like I do for Chelsea."

"I feel things too," he whispered.

That was as close to any kind of declaration either of us were going to get tonight. Talking about our feelings was like having teeth pulled. Worse. Acting on them on the other hand...

I brushed my lips over his, then lay with our foreheads touching for a few minutes. I didn't know who kissed who next, but then we were tangling tongues and clashing teeth. His stubble was rough against mine, the sensation sending a jolt of heat straight to my balls.

His hand brushed past my rapidly stiffening cock. I moaned softly against his mouth.

"Fuck, Frost." His fingers curled around me, stroking and exploring, tentative. He clearly never touched another man's cock before. I was honoured mine was the first, like his was for me.

I let my hand wander slowly down his body, over his hard chest and scarred abs. Over the tangle of hair at the base of his stomach before gripping his thick, hard length.

Slowly, we kissed while pumping each other. Neither in any hurry to finish the other, not yet. This was careful, gentle, getting to know each other like we'd never met. We might as well not have, because after this nothing would be the same between us. Did we risk ruining our friendship? We might, but neither of us seemed able to stop. Didn't want to.

"I'm going to come," Storm whispered.

"Me too," I whispered back. "Come with me."

He grunted. He preferred to give orders than take them, but his body had other ideas. He thrust harder into my hand, in rhythm with me, before we both orgasmed, cum squirting out of both our tips, and over each other's cocks and stomachs.

We both lay still for a while, hands cradling each other while our breathing slowed.

"Frosty," he said on an exhale. "I want more. Not just fucking."

"I want more too," I said. A lot more, but for now that was all we said.

I must have dozed off. When I woke again, the sun slanted through the curtains. Storm was rattling around in the kitchen making breakfast. By some miracle, Dallas actually managed to get his cock out of Chelsea.

"Is it wrinkly?" I teased.

He shot me a look before heading into the bathroom for a shower.

I grinned at Chelsea, who laughed and rolled over to face me. Storm had wiped the blood away, but the nicks on her neck stood out against her pale skin. Bruises dotted her body here and there, but she was smiling.

"Good morning, beautiful." I stroked her cheek with the back of my hand. "Did you have a nice time?"

That made her smile. "I'm not sure if 'nice' is the word. I loved every minute of it though."

My heart thumped harder in my chest. She was so fucking gorgeous she took my breath away. How could anyone not fall head over heels for this woman? I had, the moment we met. The better I got to know her, the more she became the centre of my existence. Her, now Storm.

"Me too," I agreed. "It was like... Nothing I ever did before. We didn't scare you, did we?" I didn't like the idea of tossing her in the back of the car with her head covered, but it was part of the game. Part of the scenario she consented to. The one Storm concocted and we all acted out.

"Not once I knew it was you guys," she said. "Then I could let go and let it happen." The sigh that slipped from between her lips was pure contentment.

It was the second best sound I ever heard, after her coming. I doubted anything could ever top that. Although, Storm coming was amazing too.

She tipped her head back and glanced around. "Whose place is this?"

The small house wasn't much, but it was private. We didn't have to worry about neighbours making assumptions, and calls to the police. That would have been all sorts of awkward.

"It's mine," I admitted. "I like to come here sometimes, to be alone." And daydream about bringing a woman here like this. Tying her up, or slipping her something so she couldn't fight me if she wanted to. Until now, that was all it was, a daydream. I'd never bring a woman here against her will.

Had I been tempted? I'd be lying if I said I hadn't. I had enough sense that I knew the consequences wouldn't be worth a few hours of fun. That didn't stop me from thinking about it. Fantasising while lying in bed at night, my hand around my cock.

"It's cute," she said. She pushed herself up on her elbow for a better look. One which only took a moment.

One bedroom, one bathroom and a kitchen visible through the doorway. A small lounge area off to one side. It was a tiny cottage for the twenty acres it sat on. I wouldn't have been surprised if the previous owner was a serial killer. Who else would own a house surrounded by trees, kilometres from anywhere? Just a serial killer. And me.

"You're cute," I told her. I kissed the tip of her nose.

"So are you." She kissed the tip of mine.

"Breakfast!" Storm shouted.

I winced. The cottage wasn't so big that he needed to shout for us to hear.

"I guess we better get up." I stretched my arms up over my head and reluctantly rolled over and searched for my clothes.

It was her turn to wince when she got up and started to hunt for hers. And by hers, I mean she was snatching up clothes and trying to figure out what would fit. We hadn't been gentle with her outfit last night. Most of it was now scraps of fabric, with strands of thread hanging loose and broken.

Oops.

A few minutes later, we were both dressed in a mishmash of T-shirts, track pants and underwear. I was almost certain the green boxers were mine. If not, too bad. They fit, so I wore them.

The Smashers T-shirt and black track pants were definitely not Chelsea's, but she looked adorable in the oversized clothes. Good enough to eat.

We stepped into the kitchen as Storm flipped eggs and toast onto plates and poured coffee into cups. That looked good enough to eat too. The smell made my mouth water.

"You'll spoil us," I warned.

He shrugged but didn't look over at me. "Maybe you deserve it."

"Definitely," I agreed. I snagged a plate and pulled out forks from a drawer.

Chelsea grimaced as she sat down at the table. "You wanted to talk about Atlas." She directed the statement to Storm.

"Yeah." He sat down beside me, opposite her.

Dallas, a towel wrapped around his waist, took the last chair. "Are we sharing with him too?"

"That's up to Chelsea," Storm said. He nodded towards her before shoving a forkful of eggs into his mouth.

"I like him," she said. "You think you can manage to avoid killing him?"

For some reason, she seemed to be asking that literally.

"We can try," Storm said. "Until you realise he's a stone cold asshole." He seemed certain that would be the ultimate outcome.

Personally, and in spite of everything, that was the outcome I hoped for. The guy was hot, but I couldn't see how this would work when he hated us as much as he did. And vice versa. If we couldn't get past that, we'd have a major problem. I, for one, was not walking away from Chelsea. Especially not because of him.

"One day at a time then," she said. "I have another month left of my practical placement. We all need to be professional until I'm done with that. And after that too, if the team gives me a job. Otherwise I'll have no choice but to go back to—"

"No," us three said in unison.

"We don't want you stripping anymore," I said firmly. Apparently Storm was rubbing off on me, in more ways than one.

The idea of the men leering at her, looking at her body as she took her clothes off, made me want to stab my fork into their eyeballs. Watching her dance was hot as hell and made me iron hard, but I wanted to keep that just for us. For the guys she was in a relationship with. Not for random strangers who happened to be in the club that night.

Added to that, the idea of stepping foot back in there made me uncomfortable. Before I even met Chelsea, I fucked another of the women who worked there. Ivy was pretty enough, and she got me off, but for some reason, I felt like I'd cheated. I'd seen Chelsea and I still put my dick in another woman. I couldn't have known where we'd end up, but that didn't stop me from wanting to kick my own ass.

"Not gonna happen," Storm agreed. "You're ours now. No more sharing you like that. Even if we have to tie you up here." He gave her a dark look as if daring her to contradict him.

"All the more incentive for you to behave yourselves at work," she said, scolding lightly. "Don't make my job more difficult and I have a better chance of being able to stay there."

I looked at her thoughtfully. "I kinda like the idea of tying you up here. I could stay and feed you."

"As touching as that is, I have a life I'd like to keep leading," she said. "Let's leave the tying up to times like this."

I pouted playfully. "Fine. For now." I wasn't ruling it out for the future.

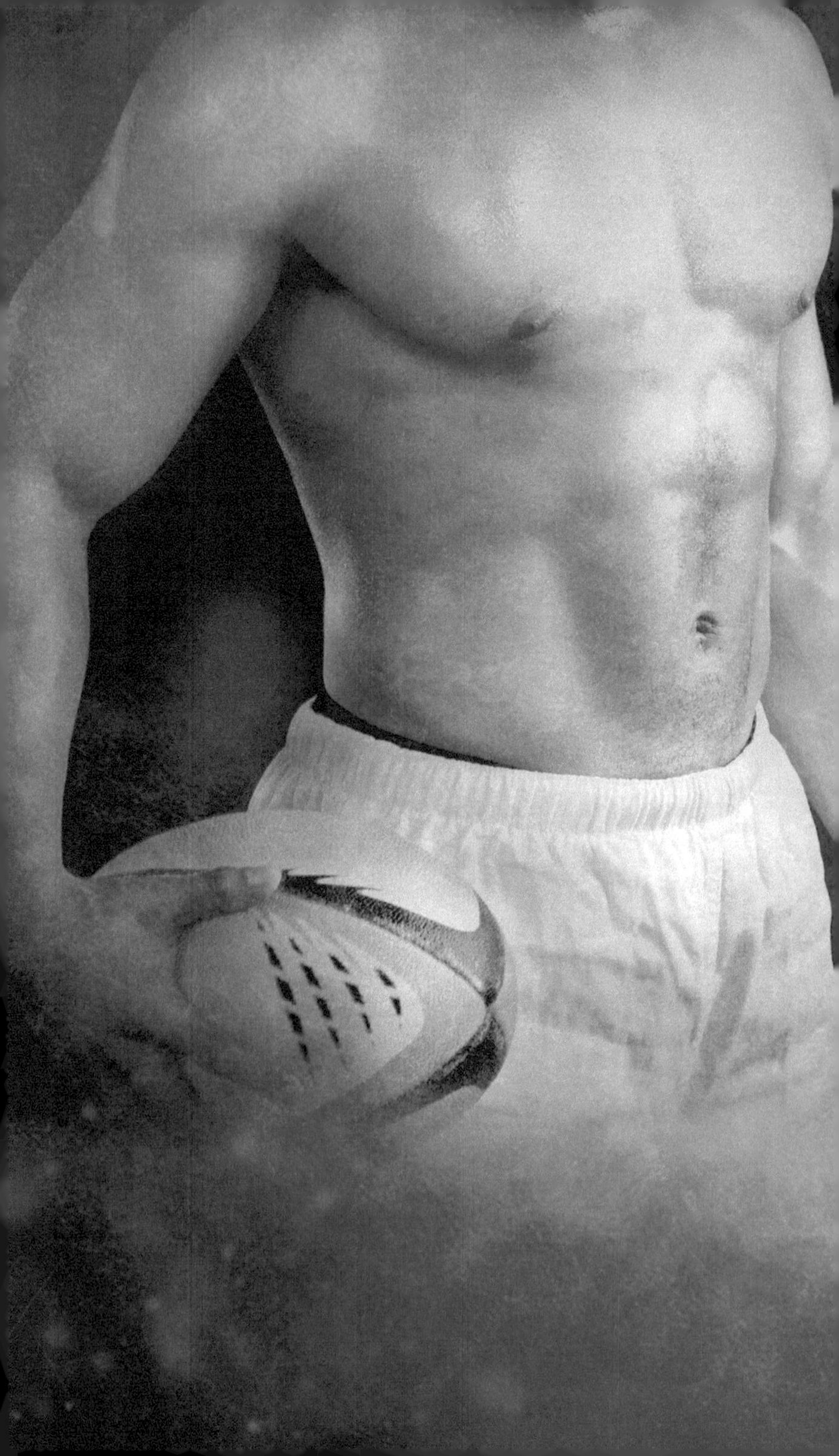

Chapter Eight

Chelsea

The guys dropped me back at my apartment and headed off to training. I decided on a long soak in the tub to loosen my aching muscles. The guys had given me one hell of a workout. Few places on my body weren't sore. I'd never been so thoroughly fucked in my life. It was absolute perfection.

After an hour, and several chapters of the romance book I was currently reading — a hockey romcom — I reluctantly dragged myself out of the bath and dried off. I stepped out of the bathroom wearing only a towel and let out a squeak.

My brother stood in the kitchen, making coffee. His back was to me, but I'd know that man bun anywhere.

He turned around and smiled. "Hey."

"Hey. You know you shouldn't break into people's apartments, right?" I eyed him meaningfully.

"I have a key." He reached into his pocket and pulled it out.

"Do I want to know how you have a key to my apartment?" I asked. I held the towel in place with one hand and waved the other in front of me. "Never mind. I'm guessing you're here for a reason?"

"I don't do anything without a reason." He turned back to pour two coffees before adding three scoops of sugar and about a quarter of a cup of milk to his.

"Are you going to tell me what it is? Is this about Belinda Simmons?" I winced. Did I want to know? "Is she—"

"Dead?" he suggested. "Yeah. She was disappointing, to be honest. I didn't think she'd give up so quickly. She's been dealt with. I know you don't want to know how."

I shook my head. "You're right, I don't." I stepped over beside him and picked up the other coffee. "Thanks."

He grinned. "What are big brothers for if they can't make their sisters coffee once in a while? And bring them good news about the problems they've solved."

"I'm not sure if it's *good* news." I ended the sentence with a sigh. "I didn't want it to come to this. If she'd just kept her nose out of my business..."

He placed a hand at the base of my neck, just above my shoulder blades. "You always had a big heart. You want people to be better. If they were, the world might be a nicer place. Boring, but nice." He ran the pad of his thumb up and down my spine. Soothing like no one else could.

"Boring isn't such a bad thing," I said.

"Boring is a terrible thing," he contradicted. "Imagine what I'd get up to if I was bored for too long. No one would be safe."

I snorted a laugh. "That's true. Are they safe now, though?"

He chuckled. "Probably not. There's only a handful of people in the world I would never hurt. You're high on the list. I can't say the same about whoever left the cuts and bruises on you." He grazed the tip of one finger across a nick on my throat, making me shiver.

"It was consensual," I said quickly. If he thought otherwise, the guys would be chained up side-by-side in his workroom. Not in an enjoyable way.

"It better be," he growled softly. "No one hurts my sister and lives to tell the tale."

"Your concern is sweet," I said, "but I'm big enough to take care of myself."

"You'll never be too old for me to stop worrying about," he said. "And taking care of. Who else is going to kill your enemies for you?"

I shivered. "Honestly, I hope the answer to that is no one." I wished the answer was that I had no enemies. I wasn't naïve enough to believe that, not exactly. They might not be my enemies directly, but rather people who'd come after me to get back at my brother, or the rest of my family.

"In reality, Mannix and Ares would help if I asked them to." He lowered his hand from my throat and picked up his coffee. "Also, I bought you a present." He nodded over to a bag on the coffee table.

"Please say that's not Belinda's head in there," I groaned. The idea made my stomach turn. I'd seen plenty of dead people at work. I didn't need parts of them at home.

He snapped his fingers. "I should have thought of that. Too late. No, I got you something else."

Warily, and with one eye on him, I stepped over to the table and gingerly opened the bag.

"Oh, you brought me pyjamas and bed socks?" I asked.

He grinned. "They have little footballs all over them. I couldn't resist."

I pulled out the purple pyjamas that were indeed decorated with tiny footballs. The socks matched. "They're adorable."

"Try them on," he said.

I'd never been shy about being naked, not even in front of him, so I dropped the towel to the floor and pulled on the pyjamas. They were warm and snug. Just what I needed after a long, hard night. The socks were soft and also fit perfectly.

"They make you look sixteen again," he remarked.

I cut him a look before returning my gaze down to my feet. "This is very thoughtful, thank you." I stepped over to kiss his cheek.

"You're welcome." He kissed mine in return. "Do we need to talk about who left the cuts and bruises on you?"

"If it keeps you from accidentally killing them," I said. I grabbed the coffee and sat down on the couch, my feet tucked up close to me. I told him briefly about Storm, Frost, Dallas and Atlas.

"It sounds like you're dating the Marvel Universe," he teased.

I smiled but flipped him off. "I think you mean the DC Universe, but Frost's first name is Daniel, not Killer."

"I've always thought Killer Ice sounded better than Killer Frost," Ice said. "Actual frost is not much more than an inconvenience. But ice, ice will kill you."

"Then your nickname is appropriate," I said.

"It's scarier than the Amazing Pyjama Giving Man," he agreed.

I giggled. "No one would ever be scared of him. He's way too silly."

"That's what he wants you to think," Ice winked. "He lures unsuspecting people with gifts of cute sleepwear, then he pounces." He mimed pouncing in my direction, like a cat.

"When you put it that way, he sounds terrifying," I said, still smiling. "Is that why you brought me pyjamas? So I'll let down my guard and bring more people like Belinda?"

He cocked his head. "I did it because I wanted to, but I guess it's kind of a thank you. She was fun. While she lasted. I wouldn't mind if you brought me more people like her. If those guys of yours piss you off, you know where to find me."

"I'm sure it won't come to that," I assured him. Or maybe I was assuring myself. "Besides, it might be difficult to make professional rugby players disappear without anyone noticing."

He placed his empty mug on the table and steepled his fingers before pressing them to his lips. "Where there's a will, there's a way. I know a guy who managed to make some high-profile people disappear during the world tour of a famous rock band. With a bit of help from the Brantley twins."

"Don't take that as a challenge," I warned him. "We want the rugby players alive, okay?" I looked at him firmly. I'd be cranky if he killed any of my boyfriends. And so would they. I saw how quickly Storm and Frost were getting close to each other while at the same time, getting closer to me. If anything happened to either of them, the other would be devastated. As would I.

"As long as they behave themselves, they have nothing to worry about," he assured me.

"Funny, I told them the same thing an hour or two ago," I said. "Dating any of them is walking a line with the team as it is. I don't want our relationship to get in the way of my job, or theirs. I care about them, but I need to secure my position with the Smashers first."

"You could go back to working at Flirts if you have to," he said. "Or better yet, I could give you money if you need any."

I gaped at him, disbelieving. "How did you know I worked there?" My face was suddenly hot. I thought I'd done a good job keeping that a secret from him and our parents.

"I keep track of my baby sister." He didn't look even slightly apologetic. "Wherever you work and whatever you do there, I like to know about it."

At least he didn't say 'whoever you do there.' That might have been followed by me throwing my coffee cup at his head.

"You don't look upset about it," I said.

"You have a beautiful body." He gestured towards me. "If you want to dance and show it off to people, why would I be upset about it?"

"It strikes me as something a guy wouldn't want his baby sister to do," I said. "Especially one as over-protective as you are." I wasn't sure if I pulled off the dark look I tried to give him. He was usually immune to my annoyance.

"I was slightly uncomfortable with it at first," he

admitted. "But then I thought about it and went to watch you one time and—"

My jaw dropped like the hinges on each side broke. "You watched me?" How did I not notice him in the crowd?

"Only for a little while. I didn't want to intrude. Long enough to see you were comfortable up there, in your own skin. Then I left. Does it bother you that I was there?"

"I suppose not," I said slowly. "I guess I should be glad you didn't drag me off the stage in front of everyone."

"I think your audience would have been disappointed if I tried." He grinned. "They were enjoying the show."

"You didn't tell Mum or Dad, did you?" I winced.

"Of course not," he said. "Dad might have taken himself down there and tried to drag you out. Him seeing you naked would be all kinds of awkward."

"That's an understatement," I said.

Top of my list of things I didn't want to have happen. Fortunately, our father didn't seem to have stepped foot inside the club. Our mother would have strangled him if he had, for one thing. Possibly me for working there too. The less they knew about that, the better.

"Anyway." He placed his hands on his knees. "I should get going. It's my turn to cook dinner tonight and I need to go and buy the ingredients to make something special."

"Some kind of anniversary?" I thought for a moment, but couldn't remember him saying anything about today's date. Granted, I couldn't remember every detail of everything, but if it was important to him, I tried to keep track.

He smiled. "No, I just feel like spoiling them. Kennedy, Mannix and Ares are three of the best people I know. You too. My four favourite people in the whole world." He leaned over to give me a hug.

"Sometimes I think you're a little unhinged, but then you go and say things like that." I squeezed him back.

"I like to keep people guessing," he said. "Sometimes I'm sweet and sometimes a little bit psycho."

"A little bit," I echoed with a laugh. Some would say he was a lot more than a little bit out of his mind. But that was part of his charm. None of us would have him any other way.

"Just a bit." He held his fingers apart as far as

they'd go. "But I want to meet these guys of yours. To make sure they're good enough for you."

"I think you'll like them," I said. "Don't go scaring them off, okay?"

His smile suggested he'd make no promises, but he wouldn't be difficult unless they were.

I waited until he stepped out of my apartment before closing and locking the door behind him. I thought about changing the locks, but he'd find a way to get another key. Plus his presence didn't really bother me, even if it was unexpected. And it was nice to know Belinda was taken care of.

Now she could only bother me in my dreams.

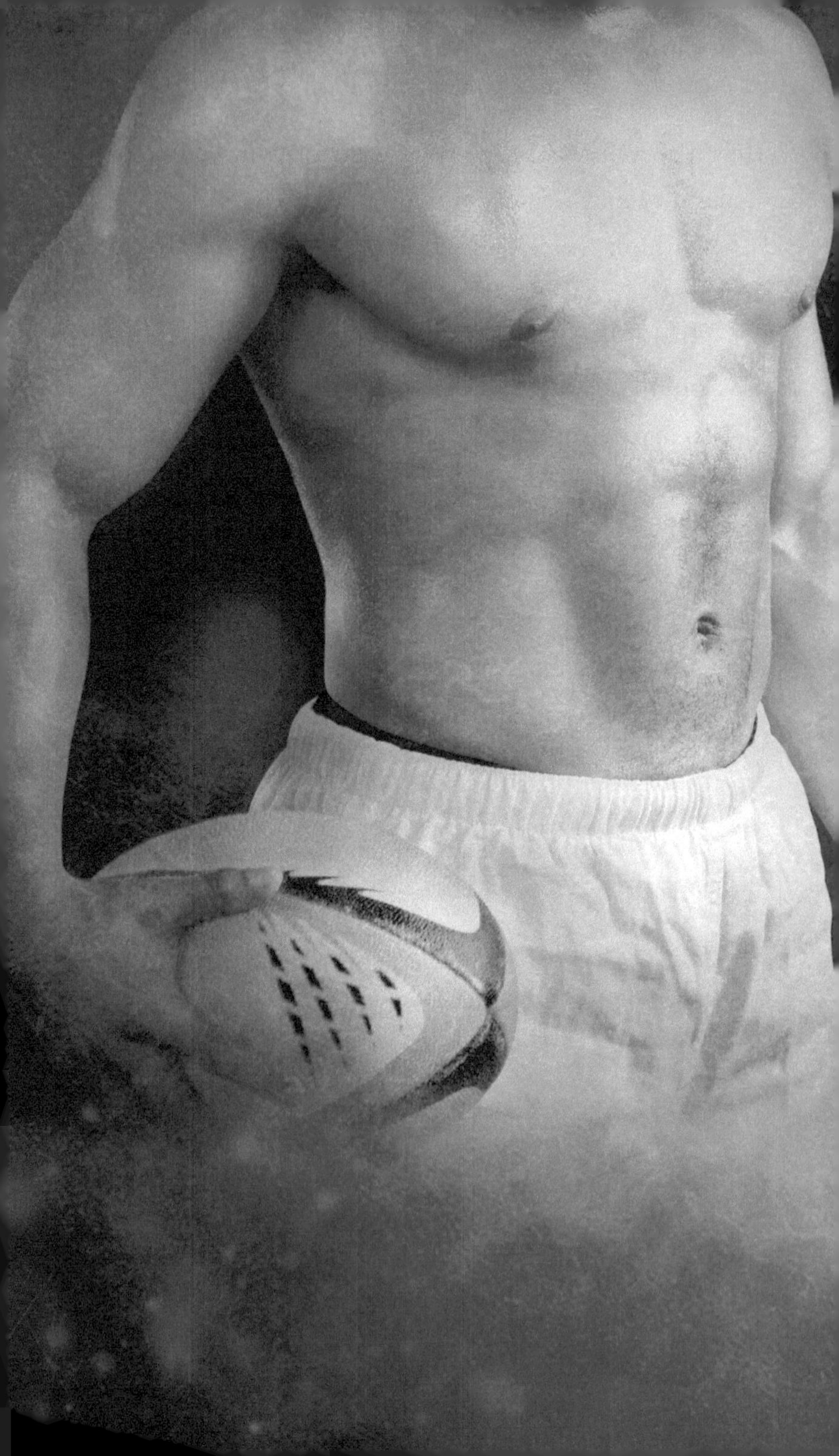

Chapter Nine

Chelsea

"This place is packed!" I shouted to make myself heard over the music and crowd at Hazards. If I had to guess, I'd say half of Dusk Bay was here.

Most of the Smashers players were gathered around the bar. Off to the side, were the Dusk Bay Demons ice hockey team and their wives and girl-friends. I spotted a few professional soccer players here and there, and a couple of members of the rock band, Ice Blue Roses.

"It'll be quieter up the back." Storm grabbed my hand and pulled me past the worst of the crowds, to an empty table at the rear of the bar. It was still noisy, but we wouldn't have to shout as loud.

I slipped into a chair. Storm claimed the one

beside me by placing his large hands on the back of it. Frost sat next to him, and Dallas opposite me.

They left the chair next to me empty. For now.

"I'll get the first round." Storm took our orders before elbowing through the crowds to get back to the bar. He returned a few minutes later, placed drinks in front of us and took his seat. Beer in his hand, he raised it to toast us all. "Here's to the last night out before the season starts."

I returned his toast and sipped my wine. "I watched your training today. You've peaked at just the right time." They hadn't missed a pass, or skipped a beat. They were so focused, I wouldn't be surprised if they didn't know I was present the entire time. They were impressive anyway, but when they were on their game, they were a pleasure to see.

"The Smashers are gonna smash everyone this season," Frost declared. "If we don't, I'll suck Atlas' cock."

"Just admit you want to do that anyway." Atlas himself flopped into the chair beside me. The glance he gave Frost was somewhere between a sneer and a challenge.

"Keep telling yourself that," Frost said. He didn't deny it.

Storm and Dallas scowled at Atlas.

"Looks like your boyfriend is jealous." Atlas jerked his thumb towards Storm.

Frost and Storm glanced at each other, but they didn't deny that either.

Storm cleared his throat. "If you're going to sit with us and spend time with our woman, you have to take part in our ice breaking ritual."

Atlas gave him a flat stare. "The fuck?"

Storm met his gaze, unwavering. "Truth or dare."

Atlas looked like he thought the fullback was out of his mind. He glanced at me, then back at Storm. "Fine, whatever." He shrugged.

"You can go first," Frost said. "Truth or dare?"

Atlas rolled his eyes. "Truth." He clearly didn't trust the others not to dare him to do something stupid.

"Let's start with something easy," Storm said. "What's your middle name?"

"Dante," Atlas said reluctantly. "Yeah, my initials are ADU, move on."

Frost chuckled. "Additional dwelling unit."

Dallas elbowed him. "What's yours?"

Frost's smile faded. "Gerald, after my grandfather."

It was Atlas' turn to chuckle.

"Mine is Elizabeth," I said. "Nothing too embarrassing, lucky for me." I raised my eyebrows at Storm. He'd started this, he might as well participate.

"Patrick," he said with no hesitation. "Also not embarrassing."

All eyes turned to Dallas, who sighed heavily.

"Ian, after my father. Yeah, my initials are DIG. No, I don't like digging."

"That was painless," Storm said. He frowned briefly. "The last time we played this, we also did truth. We shared who we lost our virginity to. As I recall, Chelsea never answered the question." He turned a raised eyebrow to me.

"Isaac!" I shot up out of my chair. I hurried around to the other side of the table as my brother pushed through the crowd to us.

As usual, he was smiling, even as he was taking in the guys sitting around the table. He gave me a hug before slipping into the last empty chair, between Dallas and Atlas.

"So, you're fucking my sister," he said cheerfully.

I'd just sat back down and took a sip of my wine when he spoke. I almost choked as the liquid went down the wrong hole. Storm and Atlas both started to pat my back. One ended up patting the hand of the other. I couldn't tell which.

"I'm fine," I said when I managed to get my breath. "Isaac, for love of fuck."

"What?" he asked, undeterred.

I shook my head at him. He was never going to be anything or anyone other than himself. No matter who he embarrassed.

"Call me Ice." He offered his hand to each of the guys in turn. "So—"

"I am," Dallas said with no hint of shame. "So are Storm and Frost. They're also fucking each other, but they don't want anyone to know yet." He ignored the looks they both gave him. "Atlas is new here. His status is currently undecided."

"Atlas wants to," Atlas said.

"Fantastic," Ice said, nodding a couple of times. "I'm a big advocate of women getting all of their needs met. For some women, that means multiple men. My girlfriend, Kennedy, she's satisfied with three. Some women need four. Or five. Or six." He frowned for a moment. "Or even seven. If that's what Chelsea needs, I'm here for it. As long as you take care of her."

"That's the plan," Storm said with a grunt.

"Seven?" Frost asked him. Then me.

"Seven is a *lot*," I said, eyes wide.

"It's an odd number," Dallas pointed out. "I don't like odd numbers."

"I do," my brother said. "My favourite number is thirteen."

"Of course it is," I told him. To the other guys I said, "That should tell you pretty much everything you need to know about my brother." It wasn't even close to everything they should know, but it would do for now. They weren't ready for anything more than that.

"I like thirteen," Frost said. "The number thirteen, not sharing Chelsea with twelve others. If we did that, we'd need a roster."

"And a shit ton of lube," Storm agreed.

"And a mountain of bath salts," I added. "I'm not going to have a relationship with thirteen men. That's too many for a girl like me to handle."

"Too fucking crowded," Dallas agreed.

Atlas nodded. "I hate to agree with Frost and Storm on anything, but I'm with them on this."

"I wasn't aware you got a vote yet, but since you agree with us, I'll let it slide," Storm said.

"I appreciate it," Atlas said sarcastically.

"Of course you do," Frost said. "We might learn to get along some day."

"What happens if you don't?" Ice asked eagerly.

He looked about ready to bounce up and down in his seat.

I glanced at him, silently warning him not to kill any of them.

He grinned, not offering me any promises if they fucked around.

"Then Atlas is out," Storm said simply, darkly.

"That's up to Chelsea," Atlas addressed that to my brother.

"Both interesting responses," Ice said. He adjusted his man bun, then left his hand at the back of his head. He leaned on it, tilting his head to the side. "I would have given the same response as Atlas if I was asked early into my relationship with Kennedy. Ares and Mannix would have responded the same way Storm did. They both had the possessive asshole thing nailed down pretty well, even then."

Atlas smirked at Storm.

"Not sorry," Storm said.

Ice grinned. "Of course not. It was just an observation." He turned to Frost and Dallas. "What would your response be?"

They exchanged glances.

"I agree with both of them," Frost said finally.

"Me too," Dallas agreed.

"Fascinating." Ice lowered his hand and rubbed his chin. "It seems like Chelsea has an interesting array of men."

"Can you stop psychoanalysing them?" I said. "I thought Ares was the psychologist?"

"He is," Ice agreed. "I guess he's rubbing off on me after all these years. Sometimes literally. He can be really—"

"Okay, you can go back to psychoanalysing them," I said quickly.

I didn't need *that* visual image in my brain. Ares was nice enough, for a grumpy alphahole, but I liked Kennedy. I didn't want to think that way about one of her boyfriends. Especially one who was like a brother to me. She was the sister I never had. Her and Sadie.

"Actually, I should get back to my family," he said. "I saw you over here and thought I'd come and say hi. So far, I approve. Don't make me change my mind." He was still smiling, but there was a warning in his eyes only a fool would ignore. Even if they didn't know what he was like, most people didn't miss the dangerous air to him. They might put it down to him being an overprotective big brother, but they knew he meant what he said. If they fucked with me, he'd fuck with them.

He nodded and stood. After a quick hug and kiss on the cheek, he disappeared through the crowds.

"Your brother is interesting." Frost followed him with his eyes until he was gone.

"That's one word for him," I agreed. I could think of a few more. Some more flattering than others. "I think it's my turn to buy a round of drinks."

"I'll get it." Dallas stood and headed off to the bar before I could make a move.

"I guess I'll get the next one." I sat back in my chair and looked around at the remaining three guys. "This has been...nice. No one has punched anyone yet."

"Yet," Atlas agreed. "According to your brother, we're all on the same page when it comes to you." Judging by the expression on his face, he was conflicted about whether that was a good thing or a bad one.

"Yeah, I got that too," Storm said. "Maybe you're all right. The jury is still out."

"Mine too," Atlas said. "I guess we'll see where things go."

"I guess so," Storm said.

I patted them both on the bicep. "How about that, you both agreed on something."

Frost pulled out his phone and took a photo of

the three of us. "To mark the occasion. Storm and Atlas being in agreement."

"It might be the only time it happens," Atlas said.

"Yeah, it might." Storm picked up the fresh beer Dallas placed in front of him and took a drink.

I smiled to myself and decided not to point out they just agreed with each other again.

This might work out the way we all wanted it to. As long as nothing else got in our way.

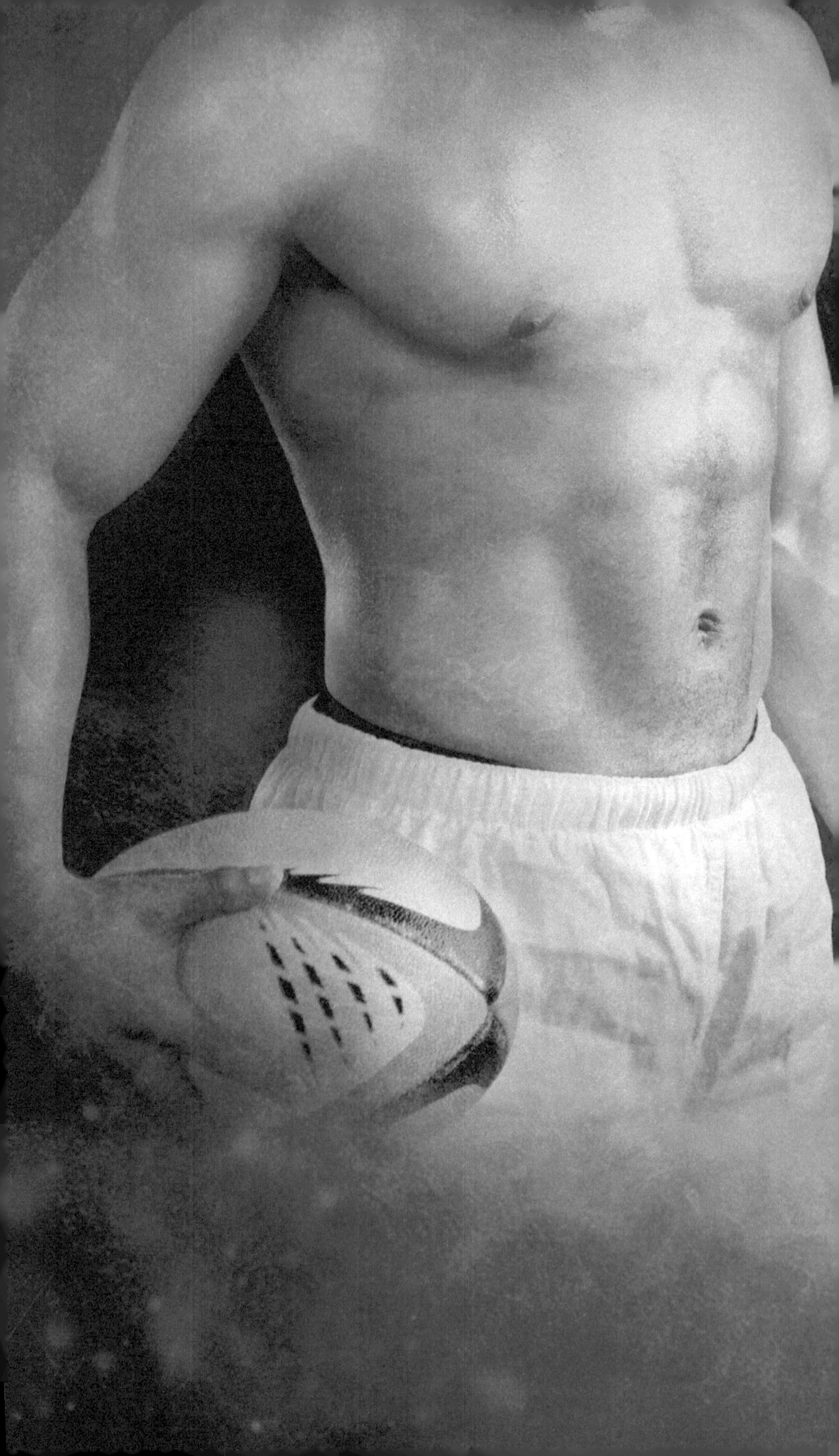

Chapter Ten

I'D HAD A COUPLE OF DRINKS BEFORE SHOVING through the crowd to go to the toilet.

"Hey." Someone grabbed my hand.

I figured they were a ruck bunny trying to get my attention and had my excuses ready.

That was until I looked over and saw Ivy, one of the dancers from Flirts. The one I fucked before getting together with Chelsea. Seeing her made me feel like a cheat all over again.

I pushed away the irrational thought, smiled as pleasantly as I could manage and pulled my hand out of her grip.

"Hi, Ivy," I said politely. "You're looking, um, nice. Excuse me, I need to go to the—"

"I need to talk to you." She stepped closer,

pressing herself to my side. Her eyes were wide, her tone a purr.

"I'm really sorry, I'm not interested." I stepped away from her.

"You were very interested that other night," she said. "I know you enjoyed fucking me." She stepped closer again. "I bet you haven't been able to get me out of your mind."

"No I haven't," I said. Not for the reasons she was implying.

"See? Come with me. Let's have a second round." Her eyes were slightly glazed like she'd been drinking or taking something. Either way, even if I was interested in fucking her, she wasn't sober enough for me to go there.

"I think you should go home." I stepped back again.

"Good idea." She put her hand on my bicep. "I don't live far from here. Let's go."

I took her hand and removed it from my arm. "I'm not going anywhere with you, sorry. Are you here with friends? Ask one of them to go home with you and make sure you're tucked up in bed."

"I'd rather be tucked up in bed with you," she purred. "Come on, I know you want to."

I shook my head. "I really don't." I started to

walk away, elbowing through the crowds until I got to the bathroom. I pushed through the door and let out a long breath.

I thought she might have left me alone, until she followed me in.

"This works too, Frosty. Can I call you that, or do you prefer Daniel?" She grabbed my cock through the front of my jeans. "I guess I can't call you anything with this in my mouth."

She started to lower herself to her knees.

I moved back so quickly I bumped my ass on the sink. "Don't." I held both of my hands out in front of me. "I said I'm not interested." What was it with this woman?

"I don't believe you." She straightened back up and pouted. "I know you want to. Guys like you always do. Why are you pretending you don't?"

"I'm not pretending." I stepped around to the side to put more space between us. "I'm flattered, but I'm with someone else."

Her eyes flashed with anger. "Chelsea fucking Miller," she spat. "What does that bitch have that I don't?"

"Me," I said. "And a bunch of other things, including respect. For other people and for herself."

Ivy raised her hand to slap me, but I grabbed her wrist before she could connect. Something in her expression made me snap. Her anger at me and at Chelsea. Anger that was completely misplaced. Whatever her problem was, she shouldn't be taking it out on my woman.

I shoved her back against the bathroom wall, crowding her in.

Triumph flashed in her eyes. "I told you—"

Whatever she was about to say was cut off when my hand wrapped around her throat. I found myself squeezing, holding her there. Her lips dropped open and her eyes started to protrude from her face. She groaned, but was unable to take a breath.

I need to stop, I told myself. *I need to stop before this goes too far*.

But I couldn't bring myself to stop. My grip had her completely under my control.

I decided whether she walked away from this or not.

I decided when she took her last breath.

I was the one with the pressure on her throat when her eyes glazed further and she slid down the wall.

My knees bending, I followed her down. My

fingers still were around her neck as I knelt in front of her, never letting the pressure go until I knew she was gone.

Only then, I lifted my hands and sagged onto my ass.

Fuck.

Fuck.

"Fuck."

I sat staring at her lifeless body until the sound of music from the bar slowly filtered into my brain. Reminding me where I was. I was in a public place and I just killed a woman.

Fuck.

I startled as the door opened, the music louder for a few moments before it closed again. Chelsea's brother came to stand beside me and looked down at Ivy.

"Seems like you need some help," he remarked.

I let my gaze slowly rise, all the way up to his face. I expected him to look horrified, but he looked calm, even curious.

"I didn't mean to," I whispered. "I swear I..." I didn't know what else to say. If she hadn't followed me... If she hadn't been so insistent... If I hadn't wrapped my hands around her throat...

If I hadn't enjoyed it.

Ice shrugged. "These things happen. I assume you had your reasons. Either way, we should get her out of here before people start asking too many questions."

I stared at him, my mouth open slightly. "You're not calling the police?"

"It's a bit late for that," he said. "She's already dead. Besides, I don't feel like answering questions tonight. I'm sure you don't either. And Chelsea would be pissed off with me if I didn't help you. The last thing I need is a pissed off sister." He seemed more concerned with that than the dead woman lying on the tiled floor.

"I don't even know what to do," I said.

"Don't panic," he said. "She followed you in and passed out drunk. We'll carry her out of here and deal with her." He pulled out his phone and shot off a couple of texts. "Just letting Kennedy and Chelsea know where we are." He crouched beside Ivy, scooping her up in his arms like she weighed nothing.

"Why are you acting like this isn't a big deal?" I asked.

"Because this is Dusk Bay. This is an average Sunday night. You'll need to open the door." He nodded towards it.

I couldn't decide if he was out of his mind or if I was. Maybe this was some kind of bizarre dream.

I opened the door and let him step out first, carrying a dead woman in his arms. He headed for the door at the back of the bar and pushed out into the alley.

"What are you going to do with her?" I asked.

"I'm going to pin this on someone who's been causing trouble for my boss," Ice said easily. "We'll make sure her family knows. And her employer."

"She worked at—" I started.

"Flirts, I know," he said. "I saw her there once. She was a talented dancer. Her family and her boss are going to miss her."

I slumped against the brick wall beside the door. "I swear, I didn't mean to do this."

"Did it feel good?" he asked. He didn't seem to be passing judgement. Again, he seemed curious.

"It felt incredible," I whispered.

He smiled. "I knew we'd get along. Next time, don't be a cliché and kill a sex worker. If you want to feel that rush again, there are much more deserving people than this."

I didn't know how to respond to that. I wanted to feel that rush again, but I couldn't go around killing people.

"What do you mean by deserving?" I followed him to his car and helped him to place her in the back of it. The way we had with Chelsea, but not bound, or with her head covered.

"If you weren't seeing my sister, I'd say people like you." He closed the back of the car with a thud. "People who kill innocent women. I mean people who do it on purpose though. People who hunt them down. You didn't take her in there to kill her, did you?"

"No!" I said immediately. "She followed me. I was trying to get away from her. I don't know why it was me she thought she wanted." Whatever she drank or took must have impeded her judgement. There would have been a ton of guys happy to go home with her if she'd asked them to. With them, she wouldn't have had to get pushy.

He put a hand on my shoulder. "You're adorable. It's a cross some of us have to bear." He sighed as though it was such a burden. "She came onto you and wouldn't take no for an answer?"

"Yeah, exactly," I said. "I told her I was with Chelsea and she got angry. Called her a bitch."

"Huh." He glanced at the back of the car. "Lucky she's dead then, I might have killed her for calling my sister that. Come on, let's get out of here."

I half-expected to be followed out of the bar, or to meet a contingent of police vehicles, but there was no one. We'd walked out of a busy club with the dead woman and no one blinked. They probably thought we were gentlemen for helping her.

Right now, I felt as far from gentlemanly as a guy could get.

"Are you going to tell Chelsea?" I asked.

"You should tell her." He got into the driver's seat. "She won't be surprised."

I shut the door behind me and stared at him, the seatbelt in my hand. "What do you mean by that?"

Had I misheard him? It sounded as though he said she wouldn't be surprised that I took a life. She was a doctor, shouldn't she be horrified?

He started the engine. "Like I said, this is Dusk Bay. Chelsea knows all about it. Like most of us who grew up here. I'm surprised you didn't know already."

"I'm not sure I know what you're saying," I said slowly.

"Dusk Bay is ruled by organised crime," he said as though that was no big deal.

"Isn't every city?" I asked.

You couldn't turn on the news without hearing about some criminal being involved in something from bribery to extortion or whatever other shit they got up to. Someone was always trying to do something to someone else. Humans had been doing it since the dawn of time. It wasn't going to end anytime soon.

He glanced over and grinned. "Yeah, but not like this. I can't remember who said it, but this place is shady shit central. Most of the businesses here are owned by, you could call them the Australian mafia. That includes Hazards and the Dusk Bay Demons, to name a couple."

"The Smashers?" Did I want the answer to that?

"Probably," he agreed. "If not directly, then indirectly."

"And Chelsea knows all of this?" I couldn't get my head around it.

"All her life," Ice said. "She even went to Brutham Academy, where they train us in careers that serve our families. She deviated a bit, of course."

"Of course," I echoed. "What do you do?" Did I want to know that either?

"For tax purposes, I'm a pathologist. I spent a lot of my time encouraging my boss' enemies to give me information. By any means necessary. That means I torture them," he added lightly. "It's a lot of fun."

"You pay tax?" I asked.

He laughed. "Yes, *that's* the takeaway here. I pay tax like you do. Probably not as much as you, though. I gather rugby is pretty lucrative, until you get too old to play. I know that won't be for a while for you, but if you enjoyed strangling Ivy, you might have a future working with me when you retire."

That should not have made my balls throb, but it did. The idea of being in control like that again... It was addictive. How long would it be before I needed another hit?

Shit, I was as bad as Dallas, just in a more dangerous way.

"I think I might like that," I said softly.

"I thought you might," he said. "Just don't practice on my sister. You wouldn't like what I'd have to do to you if I did."

I believed him when he said that. Someone who didn't blink upon walking into the aftermath of a murder was probably down for just about anything.

"I'd never harm her," I insisted. "I love her." After a moment I added, "What's wrong with me that I enjoyed doing that?"

He glanced over at me again before pulling the car into a shadowed driveway. "People like us are in touch with our darker side. Some people suppress that part of themselves. Some go into politics. Some of us kill people. I'll help you channel it in the right direction. I have a feeling you're going to learn a lot about yourself."

I had a feeling he was right and I wasn't sure if I was going to like it.

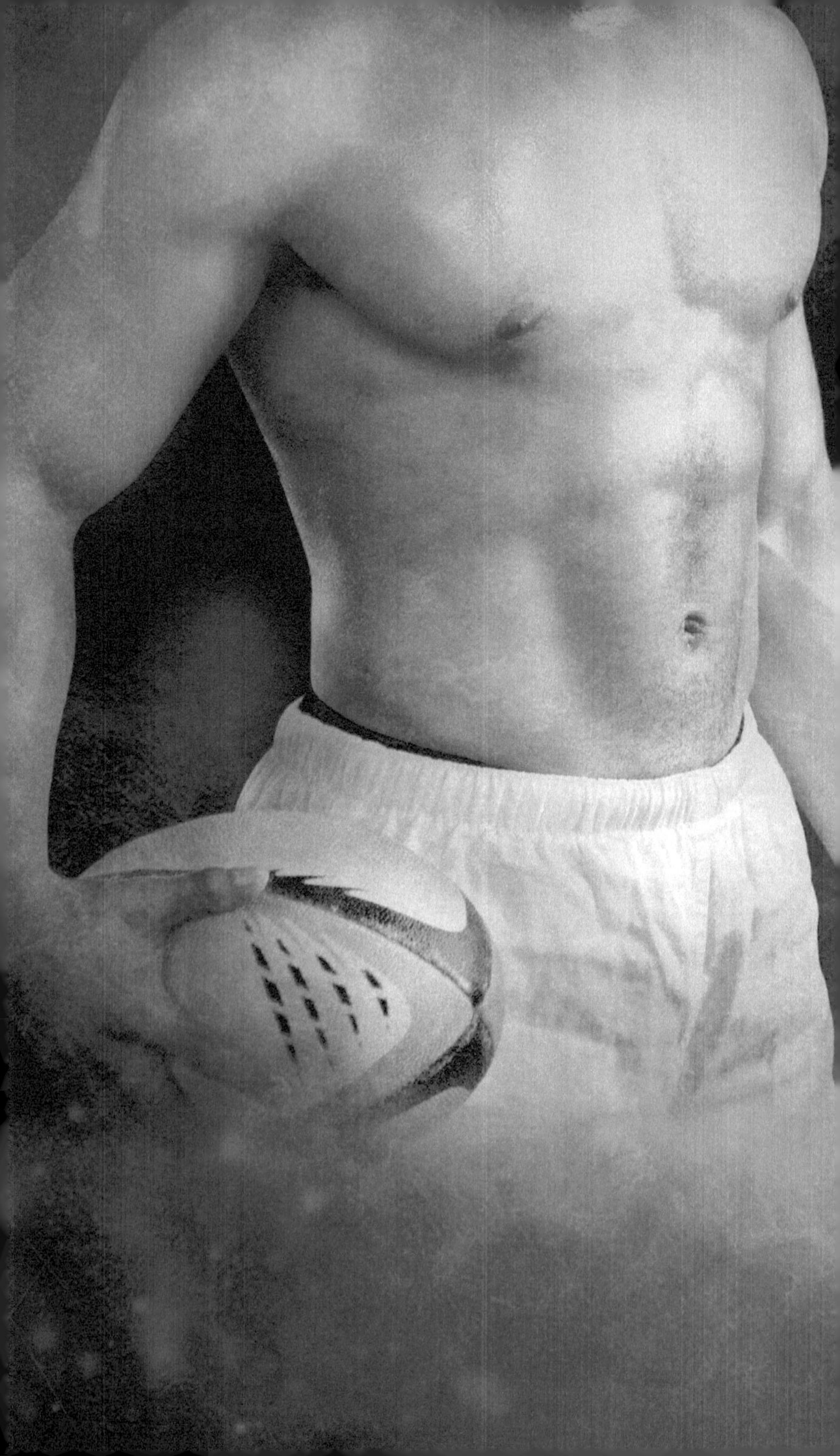

Chapter Eleven

Chelsea

After Frost left Hazards so suddenly, I couldn't sleep.

Storm insisted on taking me home and staying with me until Frost showed up to explain. Storm told the other two to go and get some rest before the morning's training session. Dallas and Atlas objected, but I insisted I was fine. Neither liked it, especially Dallas, but they left us to it. That is to say, Dallas only left so Atlas would. Otherwise they'd both have stayed, and Storm would have lost his shit.

No, it was better this way.

I made coffee for Storm and me. We sat on the couch staring at the TV without watching.

"What do you think happened?" I asked, to end the silence.

All I knew was he was with my brother, sorting something out. I had a reasonable idea of what 'something' might entail, but not what that had to do with Frost.

"Not a clue, but it better have been important," Storm growled softly.

I glanced over to him. His brow was creased, eyes like thunderclouds about to split open.

I'd never seen him look worried before.

"My brother wouldn't let anything happen to him," I said. That was the one thing I was certain of. Frost may get in over his head, but Ice wouldn't let him die. Unless he killed him. After our last conversation, I was *almost* certain he wouldn't do that.

"I don't know what—" Storm was interrupted by the sound of the key in the lock and the opening of the door.

A smile on his face, my brother stepped through. He was followed by a grim-faced Frost.

"You waited up for us." Ice stepped over to the kitchen and started to make a fresh coffee.

"We waited up for Frost," Storm said, his eyes still on his teammate.

Frost didn't meet either of our gazes. He sat in the arm chair opposite us, his head down like he carried a truck load of trouble on his shoulders.

My blood froze in my veins. I glanced at my brother who gave me a slight nod.

Fuck.

I reached over to put my hand on Frost's knee. He flinched, but didn't pull away.

"What's going on?" I asked gently. "Is everything okay?"

"Nothing is okay," he said, his face still down. "I did something."

"We all do things," Storm said dismissively. "Sometimes even things we're not proud of. If you think that will change the way we feel about you, think again."

Frost slowly raised his head. His green eyes were rimmed with red and laced with regret. "It's easy to say when you don't know what it was." His voice was barely above a tortured whisper.

"What did you do?" I asked gently.

In the corner of my eye, I saw Ice take the seat beside Frost. The irony of their matching names wasn't lost on me. Both were some of the warmest people I knew.

"You remember Ivy, from Flirts," Frost said in a hollow tone.

Storm's body stiffened. "The one you fucked. If you went there again, I'm personally going to—"

"She's dead." Frost's words cut through Storm's intended threat.

Storm frowned. "So what?"

I closed my eyes for a moment. There was no love lost between me and Ivy, but if Frost was implying what I thought he was implying... It wasn't what I expected to hear tonight.

I opened my eyes. "What happened?"

His voice breaking every few words, Frost said, "She tried to get me to go home with her. I told her no. I tried to walk away, but she insisted. And then... And then she was dead."

"It was an accident," Storm stated, as if that was that. Case closed. Move on. Nothing to see here.

Frost turned haunted eyes to him. "No accident. I wanted her to leave me alone, but then I couldn't stop myself. I had my hands around her throat, then... She was dead."

He glanced down at his fingers, curled in a strangling motion in front of him.

"Holy shit," Storm whispered. "You fucking strangled her?"

I squeezed Frost's knee. "Are you okay?"

Storm stared at me, then at him, then back again. "Are you out of your mind? He killed someone and you're asking if *he's* okay?"

"Yeah, I am," I said. "You really think he went out of his way to do it?"

The big fullback gaped. "Frost would never... Would he?" He turned to Frost. "Would you?"

"I didn't," Frost said.

"But he might in the future," Ice said cheerfully.

"Isaac." I shook my head at him.

"What? You said not to kill any of them. You didn't say anything about not recruiting them." Steam rose from the cup in his hand, dancing in front of his face before his breath dissipated it.

"I thought it was implied," I said dryly. It seemed to me like that horse had already bolted.

"I'd say sorry, but Frost was lucky I was the one who walked in and not someone else," Ice said.

"He helped me take care of her," Frost said. "He said you wouldn't be surprised about any of this."

I leaned back and rubbed my temples. "I'm not," I admitted. I'd seen the darkness in Frost, but I hadn't anticipated it would manifest in this way. "You liked it, didn't you? Killing her."

"What kind of fucked up question is that?" Storm demanded.

"A pretty standard one for Dusk Bay," Ice said. They could have been discussing the rising price of cantaloupe.

Storm looked at him like he'd completely lost his mind. "What the fuck are you talking about?"

"Ice said the whole city is run by organised crime," Frost said. "That people regularly turn up dead. He said they own everything here, including the sporting teams."

"It's true," I said wearily. This whole night had been long and I was tired.

Storm's stare turned to me. "Who the hell *are* you?"

"The same person I've always been," I said. "I grew up here. I know what the place is like. I knew it was only a matter of time before you found out. I didn't expect it to happen this way."

He looked disbelieving. "Right. I guess you weren't going to sit me down and say, hey, the fucking mafia run Dusk Bay." He nodded over to Ice. "What's your role in all of this? Are you going to tell me you're some kind of mafia don?"

Ice laughed. "No, but I work for one. They're not so bad when you get to know them. As long as you stay on their good side. If you don't, your rugby career will be the least of your worries."

"Are you threatening me?" Storm growled.

"Not threatening, just stating a fact," Ice said.

"Now you and Frost know the truth of things, you might be useful to us."

"How?" Storm demanded. "How the fuck are you planning to use Frost? Or Chelsea?"

"That's up to them," Ice said.

"I try to stay out of it," I said. "I have enough on my plate without getting involved."

Frost stared at Storm, naked fear on his face. "Ice said he'd help me to channel my feelings in a productive direction."

"What the fuck does that mean?" Storm snapped.

"It means someone who enjoys killing can be useful," Ice said easily.

"Enjoys killing," Storm echoed vaguely. "What sort of fucked up person are you?"

I bristled at the accusation aimed at my brother, but Ice only laughed again.

"That depends on the given day. Some days, I'm more fucked up than others. But I get paid for it. Just like you get paid to smash the crap out of people on the footy field. Don't say you don't enjoy it."

"Of course I fucking do," Storm said, "but I'm not killing anyone."

Ice leaned forward towards him. "Have you ever

wanted to beat the shit out of someone who deserved it? Someone who maybe, I don't know, hurt a person you care about? How would it feel to do that and not have to worry about the consequences?"

Storm shifted in his seat.

Ice leaned back. "That's what I thought. You don't have to commit to anything now, but if an opportunity like that arises, I know where to find you."

"I really should get that lock changed," I said.

Ice chuckled. "It's too late for that. It was too late when Frosty here wrapped his hands around that woman's throat. Some would argue it was too late when they met you."

I wanted to argue against that point, but I found I couldn't. I knew sooner or later it would come to this. It certainly could have been worse, Ice was right about that. Anyone could have walked in on Frost. They could as easily have killed him as helped him.

"What happens now?" Storm asked. "Are you getting the police involved? Or the team?" He quickly added, "I'll tell them Frost was with me all night."

"It's taken care of," Ice said. "No one needs to know but the four of us. And Mannix Cassani. He's the Brantleys' right-hand man here in Dusk Bay. One of them. Nothing much happens here that doesn't go through him. Don't worry though, his bark is worse than his bite. Although, his bite is pretty good." He grinned.

"Mannix is Ice's boyfriend," I explained. He wasn't the kind of person to be screwed with lightly. He'd screw back, twice as hard.

Storm rubbed the heel of his hand up and down the centre of his forehead. "Any minute now I'm going to wake up and find out this is a bad dream."

I squeezed his bicep. "It's not a dream. You don't have to do anything you don't want to do. If you prefer to stay out of things, you can." 'Things' had a way of choosing for us, but now wasn't the time to tell him that.

Storm looked at Frost past the side of his hand. "Are you going to be killing people for this guy?" He gestured towards Ice with a flick of his fingertips.

"I...maybe," Frost said. "You have no idea how it felt. It was..." He looked as though he'd experienced his first orgasm. "I felt fucking powerful. I watched her life end. I *made* her life end. Me."

"Murdergasm," Ice said. "I feel like that every time. It never gets old."

"You're both sick as fuck," Storm said. He

lowered his hand and shook his head. "I can't listen to any more of this. I need some air."

No one stopped him as he got to his feet and stomped out the door.

"He might never talk to me again," Frost whispered. His eyes widened and he blinked a couple of times. "What happens if he goes to the police?"

"I think you know the answer to that," Ice said.

Frost's face paled. "You'd kill him."

"Or you could," Ice said.

"No one is killing Storm," I said. "He's not going to the police. What would he say anyway? You've taken care of any evidence by now. If they investigate, there won't be anything to find."

"There will be, but it'll point to someone else," Ice said easily. "Even if he were to walk into a police station and admit what he did, there's nothing to prove Frost had anything to do with it."

"People might have seen her follow me into the bathroom," Frost argued.

"And they saw us carry a drunk woman out," Ice said. "Trust me, this cannot be traced back to us. I'm very good at covering the tracks of myself and other people."

"He really is," I said. "He's had a lifetime of doing it. Covering for himself and me." On paper, he didn't even have a speeding ticket. Anyone would think he was squeaky clean and innocent as fuck.

"What about Storm?" Frost asked. "What if he never accepts any of this?" In a whisper he added, "What if he hates me? Us?"

"He'll come around," Ice assured him. "You should have seen Kennedy when she first found out about all of this. She freaked out. Now, she's as involved as the rest of us. He clearly cares about both of you. He'll get past this."

"What about Dallas? And Atlas? And the rest of the team?" Frost shook his head, trying to get his thoughts in order.

"Dallas and Atlas will find out when the time is right," I said. "There's no reason anyone else needs to know. Not for now anyway."

Frost's brow dipped in a deep V. "Do the Demons know?" He directed the question to my brother. "You said the Brantley twins own them? Do they know all of this goes on?"

"Most of them," Ice replied. "The head coach is one of my boss' other right-hand men. Some of the junior coaches who used to be players as well. They either work for the team, or they work for the Brantley family in some other capacity. If the shit ever hits the fan, you'll be grateful they do. More than once they've come to the rescue."

"This is fucking wild," Frost said.

"It really is," I agreed. I glanced at the door, hoping Storm wasn't out there doing something he'd regret.

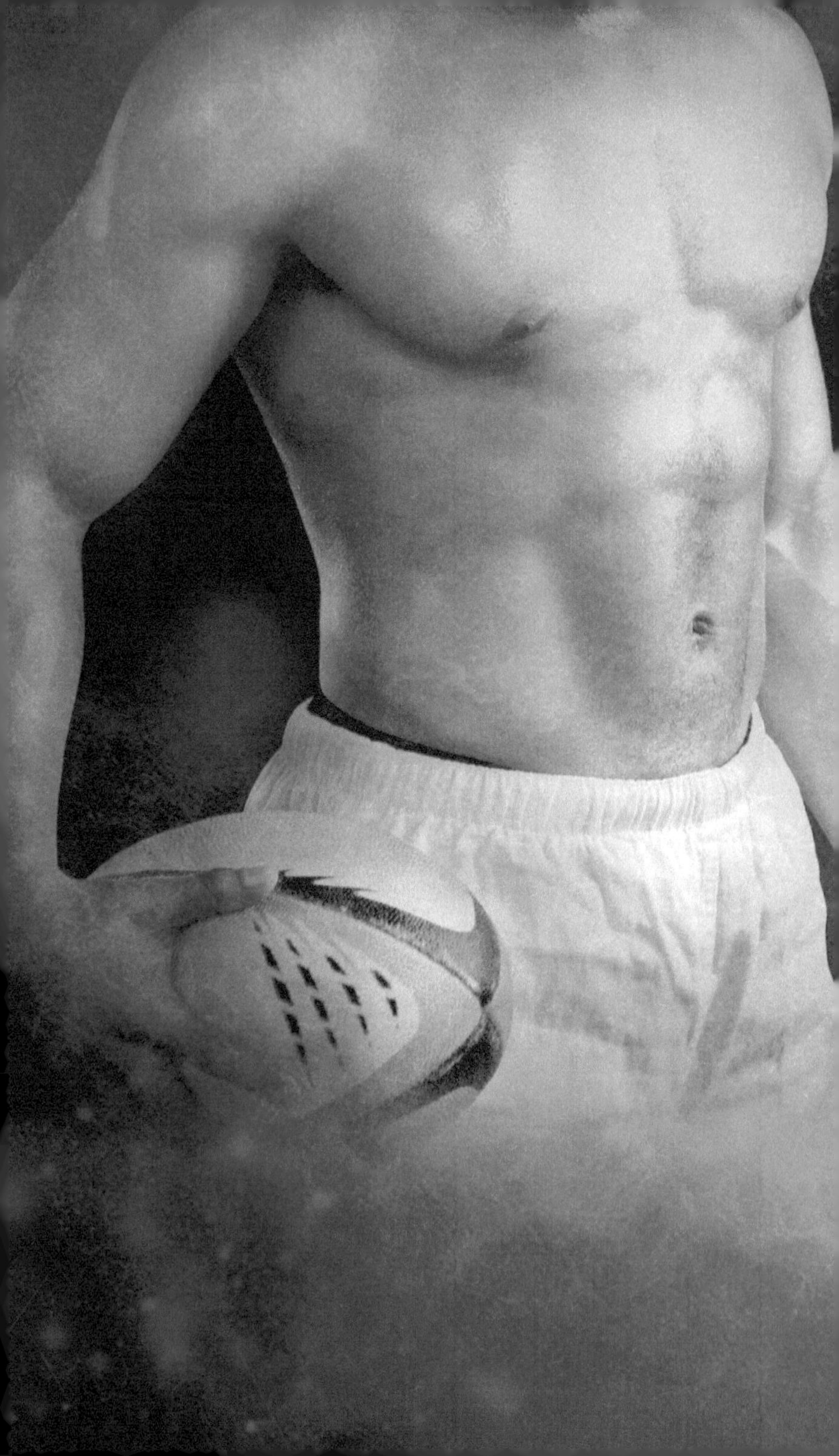

Chapter Twelve

Chelsea

After he finished his coffee, Ice left. Frost nodded off in the armchair. I waited for a while, then stepped outside to see if I could find Storm. He might have gone home, but I sensed he was close.

I headed down to the car park and found him sitting in a dark corner by himself. I almost missed him at first, but he moved, scuffing his feet on the concrete.

"Storm?" I said softly. "Are you okay?"

He grunted. "Nope. I don't know how you are."

I sat down beside him so we weren't quite touching, but close enough to feel his warmth. "I've had a lifetime to get used to it. If I just found out, I'd be packing and getting ready to get the hell out of Dusk Bay."

"Is that what you think I should do?" he asked.

"No," I said quickly. "You wouldn't turn tail and run. I know you better than that. Yes, this is strange, and it's a lot, but is it really the weirdest thing you've ever heard?"

"Yes," he said without hesitation. "My best friend, my... I don't even know what to call him. He killed a woman and liked it. He wants to do it again. It's one thing when he was slipping you a roofie, or tying you up and fucking you. What if he decides he wants you dead? What if he chokes you and can't stop himself from going too far?"

"Is that what you're worried about?" I asked gently. "I can take care of myself."

Ivy should have been able to as well, but now was not the time to mention that.

"Not if you're drugged," he argued. "You won't be able to do anything but lie there and let him kill you. Fucking hell." He raised his fist as though to punch the concrete wall beside him, but dropped it to his thigh.

"You'd be there to stop him," I said. "But I know for certain he won't do that to me. He cares about me. About us. He lost his shit once. He's not going to do it again. We'll make sure of that."

"What if we can't?" Storm asked. "He might kill me, then you."

"He won't," I assured him. "If you're so worried, we could always kill him first." I didn't mean it, but it got the reaction I expected.

"I'm not killing him," Storm insisted. "This whole conversation is fucked up. Why are we talking about killing anyone? How could he do something like that? He could have asked for help. We would have dealt with her."

"How?" I asked, curious how he'd answer in his present frame of mind.

He exhaled, loud and frustrated. "I don't know. We could have put her in a taxi, or walked her home. Something."

"She might have come on to you instead," I said.

"Then I would have—" He closed his mouth with a click.

"What would you have done?" I insisted.

He was a simmering pot, ready to boil over. I wasn't sure if he realised that. He saved the violence for the rugby field, but it was close to the surface, itching to spill over into the rest of his life. Better he realise that now before he lashed out the way Frost had.

"I would have told her to fuck off," he said.

"And if she refused?" I asked. "What then?"

"I would have walked away," he insisted.

"What if she followed?" I pressed.

"I would have—" He cut his words off again.

"What would you have done?" I pressed harder.

"I would have stopped her," he said, his voice quieter now.

"How? How would you have stopped her?" What I was getting at quickly sank into his mind. He didn't like it, but he needed to face it.

"If I had to, I would have fucking done what Frost did," he finally admitted. "I would have wrapped my hands around her throat and squeezed until she understood."

"Do you wish you'd done what he did?" I asked more gently. "You like having power. Do you want power like that?"

He pressed his hands to his face. "I don't know. I can't stop thinking about him doing it. I should go to the police, but instead I'm fucking hard."

I placed a hand on his thigh. "Welcome to Dusk Bay. The question is what do we do with the way you feel right now?"

"The answer to that should be extensive therapy," he said bitterly.

"If that's the path you want to take, I'll support

you," I said. "I'm a doctor, I shouldn't be advocating violence. But I also know there are some shitty people out there." People much worse than Ivy. "People the world would be better off without."

"What are you saying?" he asked. "Are you suggesting you will bring me some...I don't know... rapist, and let me kill him?"

"When you thought Frost forced himself on me, what would you have done? If you honestly thought he was capable of that?" I asked.

"I would have ripped his nuts off and choked him with them," Storm growled. "I would have smashed his face in."

"You would have killed him," I stated.

"For raping you, yeah, I would have killed him," Storm said. "I was pissed at him, but I knew he wouldn't go that far. Not really. If he was any other guy..." He shook his head.

"How would doing that have made you feel?" I asked.

"I dunno. Better. Asshole wouldn't have laid a finger on you again." His words were still grudging.

"If you want, you could make sure people like that don't rape anyone," I said.

"It's not that simple though, is it?" he asked. "Your brother isn't a vigilante. He works for people with an agenda. Right? Does he kill innocent people because his boss tells him to?"

That was a good question and one I was reluctant to answer. Yes, at times Ice might have had to torment someone he considered innocent. Times like that would be few and far between though. He much preferred to deal pain to those who brought pain to other people. It was his way of doing good in the world.

My tongue slid over my lips. "Not just because his boss tells him to."

Storm's head snapped towards me. "What the hell are you talking about?"

"Remember Belinda Simmons?" I asked.

"Yeah, bitch died in a car crash or some shit." He shrugged, not really caring one way or another what happened to her. She was gone and wouldn't bother him again, that was all that mattered in his book. Apparently he hadn't stopped to think it might not be a coincidence.

"No she didn't," I said softly. "I took her to my brother. She threatened to publish an article online telling the world I used to dance and fuck men for money. She would have ruined my career. All for a few dollars."

Storm let out a string of curses, each more harsh

than the last. "Fucking bitch. Why didn't you tell me?"

"I would have had to explain everything," I said. "Things you weren't ready to hear yet. I dealt with her to save us all the hassle. Specifically, my brother dealt with her."

"He killed her?" Storm asked.

"Yeah," I agreed. "He killed her for me."

"I wish you told me," he said on an exhale. "Next time, you *will* tell me. You don't go off and do shit like that by yourself. Understood?"

"You're adorable when you get bossy," I teased. It was also hot as hell. He'd gone from uncertain to possessive and aggressive in the blink of an eye. Quick enough to give anyone whiplash. He was fascinating.

He reached over to wrap his hand around my throat. "Understood?" he insisted.

Considering the conversation we just had, I should be nervous, but it wasn't. I knew without doubt he wouldn't hurt me. Not in a way I didn't like to be hurt.

"I don't want to deal with things like that by myself anyway," I said. "Not if I don't have to."

He loosened his grip. "She was really going to

publish that crap? That would have pissed off a lot of people. I'm right at the top of the list, but the rest of the team wouldn't be far behind. Frost might have slipped her a roofie, then strangled the shit out of her. If he got to her before I did."

"If either of you got there before my brother did," I said.

He would have tracked her down and sliced her to pieces if she published that article. She would have suffered worse than she already had. It would have been difficult to cover though. The eyes of Australia would be on me and her. Her going missing wouldn't go unnoticed.

Luckily for everyone, I got to her before that happened. In a way, she should thank me. Her last hours could have been much, much worse.

"He's protective of you, isn't he?" Storm lowered his hand to my lap and laced his fingers in mine.

"Very much so," I agreed. "We've always been close. Ever since we were little. If I fell and grazed my knee, he was there helping me clean it up. If I wanted to be pushed on the swings, he'd be the one to do it. The amount of times the teachers told him off at school because he was in my classroom and not his..." I smiled.

"It must be nice to have someone look out for you like that," Storm said.

"You didn't?" I asked gently.

"If I grazed my knee, it was because my older brother pushed me over or tripped me," he said. "He was the asshole who always did things and told our parents it was me. I got yelled at and grounded and he walked away laughing. Prick."

"What does he do now?" I asked.

"Dickhead died of a drug overdose a few years ago," Storm said. "That was the one thing he did that my parents couldn't blame me for. I was away in Queensland, playing. Came home to find the family in self-destruct mode. Parents divorced a year later. Since they couldn't blame me, they blamed each other. You know whose fault it was? No one's. It was just one of those shitty things that happens. I tried telling them that, but guilt and grief are heavy and loud. They couldn't hear past them."

I squeezed his hand. "I'm so sorry. That must have been terrible."

"Yeah, well, it was what it was. Probably no surprise my family was dysfunctional."

"I think the functional family is a myth," I said. "Mine has its challenges too. All families do."

"We're family now," he said softly. "You, me, Frost, Dallas. Fuck, he doesn't know."

"No, he doesn't." I wasn't looking forward to crossing that bridge. Sooner or later, we'd have to. Before any of us got in deeper.

Chapter Thirteen

Frost

I woke in the armchair, my head at an uncomfortable angle, cheek practically pressed against my own shoulder.

I was having a dream about killing Ivy. I saw her face looking up at me, eyes wide. She struggled to scream, to breathe, but I pressed my hands down harder and harder. I was the one who breathed, almost panting as the life drifted away from her. I'd jolted awake with a raging hard on.

Holding back a groan, I straightened my head slowly, like it might crack off if I moved too fast.

A moment later, Chelsea stepped through the door. Storm was right behind her.

I sat up higher. Storm didn't look like he hated me, but he seemed wary. On guard against me. I'd never seen that expression on anyone's face before, much less his. Had I suddenly become the big, bad wolf here?

"I would never—"

He cut me off by grabbing the front of my shirt and hauling me to my feet. His mouth was on mine like he wanted to devour me.

That wasn't the reaction I expected. For a moment I was so surprised all I could do was stand there. But then, I was kissing him back, our tongues thrusting against each other for dominance. I pulled mine back, letting his invade my mouth.

When we finally pulled apart, I stared into his stormy grey eyes. "Does this mean you're not pissed off at me?"

"Chelsea explained a few things," he said slowly. "She made me see some stuff I hadn't considered before." He sucked in a breath and exhaled while saying, "I was pissed off because what you did, you did without me. You should have come to me. Texted me and told me to get my ass into... I dunno, wherever you were."

"I panicked," I admitted. "If it wasn't for Ice, hell if I know what I would have done." I might have called the police and told them everything. Or I might have run. I had no idea. He was right though, I could have included him. Or at least, tried.

"You might have panicked too," I said finally.

He was still gripping the front of my shirt, and now he shook me slightly. "When have I ever fucking panicked?"

"When have you been faced with a dead woman?" I shot back. "I had no way of knowing what you'd do. I don't know what I would have done if the tables were turned."

"Yes, you do," Chelsea said. "You would have stood by Storm, or me. You're the kind of guy who helps his friends to bury the body."

I grinned uncertainly. "I am, aren't I? Is this where you tell me you have bodies you need help burying?"

She snorted. "Not this week. I'll let you know though."

"You better let us both know," Storm growled. "We're in this together."

"What about the others?" I asked tentatively. "Dallas is going to figure things out sooner or later." I was surprised he wasn't here right now, wanting to slide his cock into Chelsea. Needing to.

Was there a single one amongst us who wouldn't benefit from extensive therapy? I didn't think so.

"I have an idea," Chelsea said. "Let me work on something. We'll all let him know what's going on together. Atlas too."

"I'm happy to tell Atlas," Storm said. When we looked at him, confused, he added, "If he doesn't like it, we can kill him." He didn't seem to be joking.

"You know you can't go around killing everyone who disagrees with you," Chelsea said.

Storm gave her a flat look. He clearly didn't agree with that statement.

I started to wonder if I created a monster here. Maybe, but I couldn't quite bring myself to regret it. What I did to Ivy, it was addictive. I couldn't stop thinking about it. At some point, I'd want another hit. Not tonight, maybe not this week, but someday.

If I could bottle the sheer power, I'd be a billionaire.

"Let's hope it doesn't come to that," I said. I also hadn't put the idea of sucking Atlas' cock out of my head. In the meantime, there was only one cock I wanted to suck. If he'd let me.

I pulled Storm's hands off the front of my shirt and slowly knelt down in front of him. Giving him the chance to step away or say no. Tentatively, I looked up at him.

Would he reject me, or was he as down for this as

I was? He'd only found out an hour ago I killed a woman. I'd understand if he didn't want to rush.

He regarded me with half-lidded eyes before he finally nodded. Decision made, he looked eager now. Ready.

I undid the front of his jeans and opened them. His cock sprang free, bobbing in front of my face. Engorged and thick. His tip was quickly slick with pre-cum.

"I've never done this before," I admitted.

"You can't do it wrong," Chelsea said. She sat on the floor beside me and undid my jeans to free my own erection. Her eyes on me, she leaned down to take me into her mouth.

Fuck, her mouth always felt like pure heaven. Would mine feel like that to Storm? That thought almost made me come down her throat, then and there. I blinked a couple of times, trying to clear my head and slow the flow of blood enough to regain control. Knowing I was a killer was one thing. I'd never recover from being a one-pump chump.

Priorities.

Copying Chelsea, I licked the head of Storm's cock, tasting his pre-cum and savouring the guttural groan that slipped from between his lips. Encouraged, I teased him with the tip of my tongue before placing my lips as far down his length as they could reach. So far, he tapped the back of my throat.

At the same time, I kept trying not to come too fast from the treatment Chelsea was giving me. That was getting harder and harder. Literally. She was leaning down low, her back arched like a cat, blue eyes on both of us.

"Panther," Storm whispered.

I looked from him to her, to see her eyes smiling. It must be something between them. I'd try to remember later so I could ask them about it. It seemed appropriate though. With her dark hair and flexible body, she could have been a big cat. A beautiful one, too elegant to be caged.

When she cupped my balls and started to massage them, I did the same to Storm. I decided she was right; I couldn't do this wrong. Storm looked like his eyes were going to roll back in his head with bliss. As for me, I loved the way he felt and tasted, smooth and hard at the same time. Velvet skin over rigid steel.

I struggled to hold on, but I couldn't stop myself from coming, frantically fucking Chelsea's mouth, my cum painting the back of her throat before she swallowed.

She slid off me as Storm pulled me off his cock

with a pop. He grabbed both of our hands and pulled us to the bedroom. Somehow we made it to the bed, Chelsea's mouth on Storm's cock while I dove down between her legs.

She tasted as good as he did. Maybe better. Or— No, I wouldn't make a comparison. They both tasted amazing. Perfect.

She was so slick, my tongue slid against the entrance to her pussy and over her swollen clit. She was always so ready, so willing. Even when I drugged and fucked her, she was wet. I've never met a woman who liked sex as much as she did. As much as I did. She couldn't get enough and neither could we.

I pushed my tongue inside her as deep as it could go. Fucked her with it a couple of times and savoured her moans of appreciation. They matched Storm's as she sucked on his cock, gagging every few thrusts.

My tongue still on her clit, I pushed my fingers inside her wet heat, stroking her insides and feeling her tense more and more around me. Closer and closer to coming.

I watched her carefully, seeing her reaction when I found her sweet spot deep inside her. Right there. I stroked it with my fingertips, revelling in the way she quivered at my touch. She was so beautifully responsive, but never more so right than now. With me touching her exactly where she needed and deserved to be touched.

She slid her mouth off Storm's cock as she came, hard and fast, drenching my fingers with her release. She was still panting when she closed her lips back over him and sucked once, twice, before he came buried inside her mouth.

He grunted and ground against her, groaning long and slow before he finally sagged down on the mattress with him, his damp cock dangling between his thighs.

I won't lie, part of me wished he'd come in my mouth, but letting me suck him at all was a huge step forward. For both of us. There was plenty of time for the next step.

I hoped.

Chapter Fourteen

Chelsea

"IT SOUNDS LIKE THEY TOOK THAT BETTER THAN I thought they would," Sadie said, her eyes wide. "Maybe I shouldn't be surprised. They seem full of pent up violence."

"All the best people are." I gripped her ankle and touched up the nail polish on her big toe before moving onto the next one. She was so ticklish, she'd pull away from me if I let her. "I like this shade of red."

"It's pink," she said.

I squinted at her nail. "No, it's definitely red." It was a bright shade, just lighter than the colour of fresh blood.

She laughed and picked up the bottle. "It's definitely pink, look at the colour name."

I glanced over and read out loud. "Infinite purple. Who comes up with these names? It's definitely not purple."

"Yeah, but it's also not red." She cut me a sly smile.

"I think what you meant to say was it's not pink." I dipped the brush into the bottle and swiped it a couple of times before starting on her third toenail.

"I think we can both agree it's not green," she said with a laugh.

I glanced up at her and grinned. "I think I want to say it is green, just to see what you'll do."

"You're such a brat," she teased. "Speaking of, how many boyfriends are you up to now?"

"We still haven't discussed the whole boyfriend-girlfriend thing," I said, with a hint of frustration. "I'm seeing four of them, currently. But when Dallas and Atlas find out what's going on, I might be down to two."

"You poor thing." She clicked her tongue.

Playfully, I swiped the brush across the top of her foot, leaving a line of polish.

"Hey!" she protested. "You're supposed to paint my nails, not my foot. That tickled."

I glanced up. "Sorry, not sorry." I started on the

fourth nail, careful because the last two were so small.

"That was what I figured," she said. "Did I mention you're a brat?"

"It's one of the things you like about me," I retorted. "And vice versa. Now, would you keep still? I wouldn't want to accidentally get nail polish where it shouldn't be."

She used to finger quotes while saying, "Accidentally."

"Exactly," I said as though being literal. "You want me to do a good job or not?"

"I do," she said. "No one does my nails like you do. You might have missed your calling. You should have been a nail technician."

"I'll bear that in mind, if this medicine thing doesn't work out," I said.

It wasn't a bad idea if things went to hell. There was no way the guys were going to let me go back to dancing. They'd probably tie me up in Frost's cabin for the rest of my life before they allowed me to strip for strangers again.

"Painting my nails must be much more satisfying than saving people's lives," she joked. "If I could afford it, I'd pay you to do them every couple of days."

"If you could afford it, I might let you," I said. "Then I could spend the rest of my days on the couch with a good book." Or on my bed with one of the guys' faces buried between my thighs. There were worse fates.

She sniffed. "I'd have to find something else for you to do. You could be my personal physician and nail polisher."

"Where do I sign?" I lightly blew on her drying nails before grabbing her other ankle and starting to work on those nails.

"I'll speak to my team of lawyers." She leaned against the couch cushion. "We should do these spa days more often. It's so relaxing." She took a sip of champagne from the glass in her hand.

"It's a nice break from how hectic everything has been for the last while," I agreed.

I only had a week left in my practical training before final exams. After that, the real work started. Applying for jobs while hoping like hell the Smashers hired me. Or searching around for a practice I could work in while I waited for an opening on a team somewhere.

"What are you going to do if you can't find a job in Dusk Bay?" she asked. "Will you be looking for somewhere to set up a nail salon?"

I snorted. "Maybe. I think I'd have to go back to school for that though. How long does it take to get a qualification in nail technology?"

"Probably less time than medicine," she said. "That was your first mistake. If you'd gone straight to nail school, you'd be an owner of your own salon by now. Knowing you, you'd have a chain of them." She held up a hand in front of her. "I can see it now. Chelsea's Nails, in pink neon."

"Or red neon," I said, nodding towards her nails.

"Being colour blind might be problematic," she teased. When I made to wipe polish across her other foot, she laughed and held her hand over the top of her foot. "I'm kidding, kidding. It is close enough to both pink and red to be confusing."

I gave her the side eye. "Let's go with that. In answer to your other question, I don't know what I'll do. Maybe go and work with my brother."

"You always say you wouldn't do that," she said softly.

"I don't want to," I said. "I love him and all, but I'd prefer to leave the killing to other people."

"You really think Storm and Frost are those other people?" She kept her voice down like we might be overheard in our own apartment.

"I know Frost is," I said. "How did Divina take the news about what happened to Ivy?"

Sadie pressed her lips together. "She's organising a memorial for her. And raising funds for Ivy's family. I don't think she misses her, exactly, but she respected her. You know?"

"I do," I agreed. "Ivy was good at what she did. She was gorgeous and the clients adored her." I remembered watching her and Frost step out of the private room. There was no hint of jealousy. We weren't together yet, and it wasn't as though he could ever fuck her again. He made sure of that. It was just a thing that happened in the past, that was all.

"Yeah, they did," Sadie agreed. "Even though I got the impression she thought she was better than everyone else. I never really got that. All of the dancers there are different, with different looks and different talents. The kind of guys who went for you usually weren't the kind who went for her. There was plenty to go around."

"I guess some people feel the way they feel, even if it makes no sense." I blew on the other nails and put her foot down before checking the first set of nails to see if they were dry.

"I suppose so," she agreed. "It's a shame, because

you two might have gotten along if she gave you a chance."

"We'll never know," I said. I screwed the cap back on the nail polish before setting it aside on the coffee table.

"That's true," Sadie said before we swapped spots, her on the floor and me on the couch. She picked up the colour I'd chosen for my nails. A deep red that couldn't be confused with any other colour.

She cocked her head and peered at the bottle. "Nice shade of blue."

I picked up a cushion and threw it at her. It hit her on the arm before plopping to the floor.

"I'll give you blue," I growled playfully. "As if I'd ever have that on my nails." I'd wear blue, sure, but not painted on.

"That sounds like a dare to me." She opened the red and started to apply it to my toenails.

"Remind me not to play truth or dare with you," I teased.

That reminded me of Storm, who kept bringing the game up. It was fun, but I was never going to answer *that* question. I'd take it to my grave first. Not that I was ashamed of it, but it was private. A night between two people, not something for the world to know. Not even guys I cared about.

"Next thing you will say you won't play Kink Or Drink with me," she pouted.

"I'll absolutely play that with you," I assured her. "As long as you bring your own men." I didn't need to remind her what would happen to her if there was any drama between me and her over my guys. Just like she wouldn't have to remind me to keep my hands off anyone she was seeing. Sisters before misters and all that.

"You're on," she said. "Remember the time we played that at Flirts with a bunch of clients and staff?"

"That was fun," I said. I earned a fortune in tips that night. And had a lot of fun with the raunchy card game. Invented at Brutham Academy by the Brantley twins, it was a particular favourite with me and my friends.

"Are you sure you won't come back to Flirts?" Sadie asked. "You look like you miss the place."

"I miss the people and I miss dancing," I said. "I don't miss anything else about it. It's my past now and I want to focus on the future. Right now, that consists of sitting still so you can finish my nails."

"It's unfair you're not as ticklish as I am," she complained. "Why do I have to suffer?"

"You're just unlucky in that regard," I said.

"You're lucky in other ways. You're smart, beautiful and cute. And most of all, you have me for a best friend." I batted my eyelashes at her.

"That last one almost makes it worth being ticklish," she said sweetly.

Together we said, "Almost." Then we laughed.

"Seriously though, I'm glad we're friends," she said. "You're pretty awesome. And I'm looking forward to all those free tickets to the Smashers' games."

"I knew you were my friend for a reason," I teased. "You were waiting for footy tickets."

"That's what they call playing the long game," she said. "I knew if I hung around long enough, I'd get free tickets to *something*."

"Remind me to only apply for jobs with cricket teams," I said, knowing she didn't like the sport.

"If they were free, I'd go," she said. "Anything that involves guys playing with their balls. Or a puck. Or a shuttlecock. I'm not that picky."

"I figured that out about you," I said. "That might bring us back to you choosing me for a friend."

"When it comes to friends, I'm very picky," she said. "Nothing but the best for Sadie. Sadie has the best taste in friends."

"Does Sadie often talk about herself in third person?" I teased.

"In her head, she does," she laughed. "Now it sounds like I'm weird, or crazy."

"If you are, you'd fit in perfectly with me and everyone I know," I said. No wonder there were so many psychology practices in Dusk Bay. They must be making a fortune from people like us. Like a cottage industry that grows up around various professions. Maybe they should have named it Fucked Up Bay.

"Finally, I get to fit in." She pumped a fist in the air in triumph.

"If I ever made you feel like you didn't fit in—" I started.

"You didn't," she said quickly. "You've always made me feel included and loved. Like you do with everyone around you. It's one of your superpowers. Mine is the ability to chain pour twenty drinks in a row."

"That's a useful skill," I said. "Especially on a Saturday night."

She laughed and leaned down to concentrate on painting my nails.

Chapter Fifteen

Chelsea

I WINCED AS STORM SLAMMED THE OTHER player down to the grass. Some days, I swore I could hear bones strain with the effort not to break. Other days, the strain was too much and the moment they snapped was obvious and painful.

On this occasion, both players jumped straight back to their feet, attention still on the training session.

"I remember being that young," Doctor Stuart remarked.

I glanced over at him and smiled. "You're not that old."

He chuckled. "We both know that's not true. It's been a long time since I was out there on the field, playing."

"You used to play rugby?" I straightened my ponytail and kept my eyes on the training session.

"I did, and I was good at it," he said. "I could have given any of those boys a run for their money back in the day. I could have played for Australia, but my wife didn't want me to. We had young children and she was scared I'd get injured. Besides which, there wasn't money in playing back then. Not like there is now. I was trying to juggle that and seeing patients. Working for the team like this was a compromise."

I glanced over at him quickly. "How many kids do you have?"

This was the first time he mentioned any. We were usually so busy we didn't get a chance to talk about anything personal. Our conversations consisted of comparing notes about particular players, to make sure the whole medical team was on the same page with their treatment. Every cog in the wheel had to be in place for it to run smoothly.

"Four," he replied. "Not one of them is a doctor." He clicked his tongue, but didn't stop smiling. He was definitely not the sort of person who would insist their child follow in their footsteps just to satisfy them. He'd want them to decide for themselves.

I patted him on the shoulder before looking back to the field. "I'm sure you're proud of them anyway."

"Absolutely, I am," he said. "My oldest is an engineer. The middle two are both teachers. My youngest is a graphic designer."

"Do any of them live in Dusk Bay?" I asked. I wondered if he knew what the city was really like. I got my answer when he cut me a look.

"No, they don't. They're spread out all over the country. Living their own lives, with their children." The response was careful, as unsure of what I knew as I was of him.

"You must miss them," I said, deciding to sidestep the direction the conversation might take. Unless I completely missed my guess, his approach was like mine. Aware of what was going on, but trying his best to keep his nose right out of it. For the benefit of our working relationship, it was better not to get into it.

"I do," he said. "I admit, that's one of the reasons I enjoy working with you. You remind me of my kids. Smart, respectful and determined. Your parents must be very proud of you."

"I like to think they are," I said. "They will be when I'm actually working as a doctor."

That was a not-especially-subtle hint. This was

the last day of my practical training and Doctor Stuart hadn't said anything about recommending me to the team.

"I'm sure they will," he said, his tone suggesting he was trying to get a rise out of me.

I tore my eyes away from the maul on the field and looked at his smile. I raised my eyebrows at him.

His smile widened, making the lines around his eyes crinkle. "You know I don't make the final decision."

"I know," I said carefully.

"But I gave my recommendation to the general manager a couple of days ago." He turned his gaze back as Frost took off across the field with the ball.

"Oh." I focused on Frost and his powerful legs as he ran and threw himself over the try line.

The man had thighs that would pulverise a watermelon. They all did. Watching them pumping as they flew across the grass was hot as fuck. An image of Frost on his knees, his mouth on Storm's cock, made my clit throb. The wet sound of him sucking was better than the roar of the crowd on grand final day. Better than music. The taste of his cum still lingered on my tongue. Salty and delicious.

I finally managed to say, "Thank you. I appreciate that." I really did, but until the GM asked to see me, everything else was up in the air.

As if he read my mind, Doctor Stuart said, "Bruce mentioned something about interviews in a week or so. I'm sure he'll include you in them."

He spoke lightly, but there was nothing definite in his tone. He didn't have a say, but he was trying to be reassuring in the best way he knew how. He wasn't given to beating around the bush, as they say. He couldn't afford to be. None of the players would respect him if he wasn't honest and clear with them. Not to mention authoritative. He had years of experience telling big, stubborn men what to do.

In spite of his words, my heart sank. Of course I didn't think I was the only candidate for the job, but clearly I hadn't given it enough consideration. There must be dozens of doctors better qualified than I was. People with years of experience working with athletes. Why the hell would they choose someone straight out of university?

I felt as though my dreams were slipping through my fingers like water.

"If he doesn't, there will be other opportunities." I tried to smile, but my own words felt hollow.

I was twenty-five. I had friends who had their shit together. They were living their lives, getting married and having babies. Working in their chosen careers, or at least jobs that paid the bills. Suddenly I felt like I was clinging to a life raft that was hurtling down a river with no end.

I reminded myself rivers always had ends, but since they fed into the expansive ocean, maybe that wasn't such a great analogy.

"Have they ever hired anyone that did practical training with the team?" Did I want the answer to that? Not really, but the question was out there, I couldn't shut it back in its box.

"Not to date," Doctor Stuart said. "But this is a different situation. The season is about to start and we're still down a couple of doctors."

He was in charge of all things medical for the team, but several others worked under him. Medical specialists, like I hoped to be; physical therapists, dieticians and whatnot. If we didn't have everyone we needed, the team might suffer.

"I'm sure that will be rectified quickly," I said. If the GM was conducting interviews, those positions would be filled. I just desperately wanted to fill one of them.

"It has to be," Doctor Stuart said. "Are you certain this is what you want? You realise you have to be on call twenty-four hours a day, seven days a week. Travelling with the team everywhere they go. On the sidelines, waiting, in case someone is injured. It can be intense."

"That sounds perfect," I said. "I'm ready to commit myself to the Smashers, and everyone who works for them, and with them."

My practical placement focused on getting to know the team and watching them in action, but working for them, I'd be seeing the staff and their families as well. The team looked after everyone involved with them. Like one big family.

"I believe you," Doctor Stuart said. "That was why I gave Bruce my recommendation. If he knows what's good for him, he'll hire you." He nodded like he might scold the general manager if he didn't take his recommendation. To be honest, it wouldn't surprise me. Doctor Stuart was like a father to most of the team. Why wouldn't that include the GM?

"It doesn't hurt that so many on the team like you," Doctor Stuart added. "And that you know how to be discreet."

I glanced over at him, taken by surprise by his words. Mortified. "I don't know what—"

He chuckled. "I might be old, but I'm not stupid. Some of those boys hang around more than they did before you started here. I've seen the way they look at you. I've also noticed your hair out of place after some of the visits."

My face heated. That didn't sound like I was being discreet at all. I should have realised he was paying attention. Of course it was, it was his job. What the hell must he be thinking of me? That I was wildly unprofessional, most likely. Which wasn't far from the truth. I should have been better at setting boundaries with the guys. Not fucking them in the treatment room. This could easily end all my hopes. My heart raced and sweat sprang up on my palms and under my arms.

Without thinking, I patted my hair. "I know I shouldn't, but..." What else could I say about it? Everything I worked for was in his hands right now. If he was about to withdraw his recommendation, I'd be gutted. He wasn't someone the guys could just deal with to keep quiet either. He was a good man and the team needed him.

"I was young once," he said. "As long as you keep it discreet, I see no reason for it to become a problem. People on the team have relationships with each other all the time. If it interferes with the team winning, that's one thing. They seem to be more cohesive recently. You might be a good influence, or no influence at all. Either way, things haven't gone backwards. As long as they don't, then I'll keep my nose out of it."

"If it interferes with the team winning, I'll kick their asses myself," I growled. I wouldn't hesitate. Although Storm would do plenty of kicking of his own. The others too, but him in particular. He was happiest when he was in control. Including making sure the team succeeded.

"I thought you would," Doctor Stuart said. "They might not want you involved with the team on a full-time basis though."

I frowned. "What do you mean?" Had any of them said anything to him about me? If they had, they might look forward to having more than their asses kicked.

"I mean there are times when I've missed birthday parties and special occasions because I've been called out," he said. "My wife was not impressed. Fortunately for me, she never asked me to choose. I would have missed her." He chuckled.

"Anyone you get involved with is going to have to understand the job comes first. They'll want to celebrate a win while you're setting a bone. Or treating a concussion. Or in a meeting with the other medical staff to make a plan for a particular player. This job is never boring."

I noticed that the moment I stepped foot in the stadium. Even when the team wasn't present, there was a buzz in the air. Staff were all busy doing something, from preparing the grass, to booking entertainment in the off-season. Just because it wasn't footy season, didn't mean we got to switch off. I loved it. Everything in me itched to be a part of that. I wanted to be one of those people who were here so long others joked they were practically part of the furniture. An integral part of the team, like the logo.

"They'll understand," I said. The team was important to all of us. We'd find a way to work it out.

"They might, they might not," he said with a shrug.

A second or two later, we were both sprinting out onto the field as a player landed heavily, groaning in pain and clutching his leg.

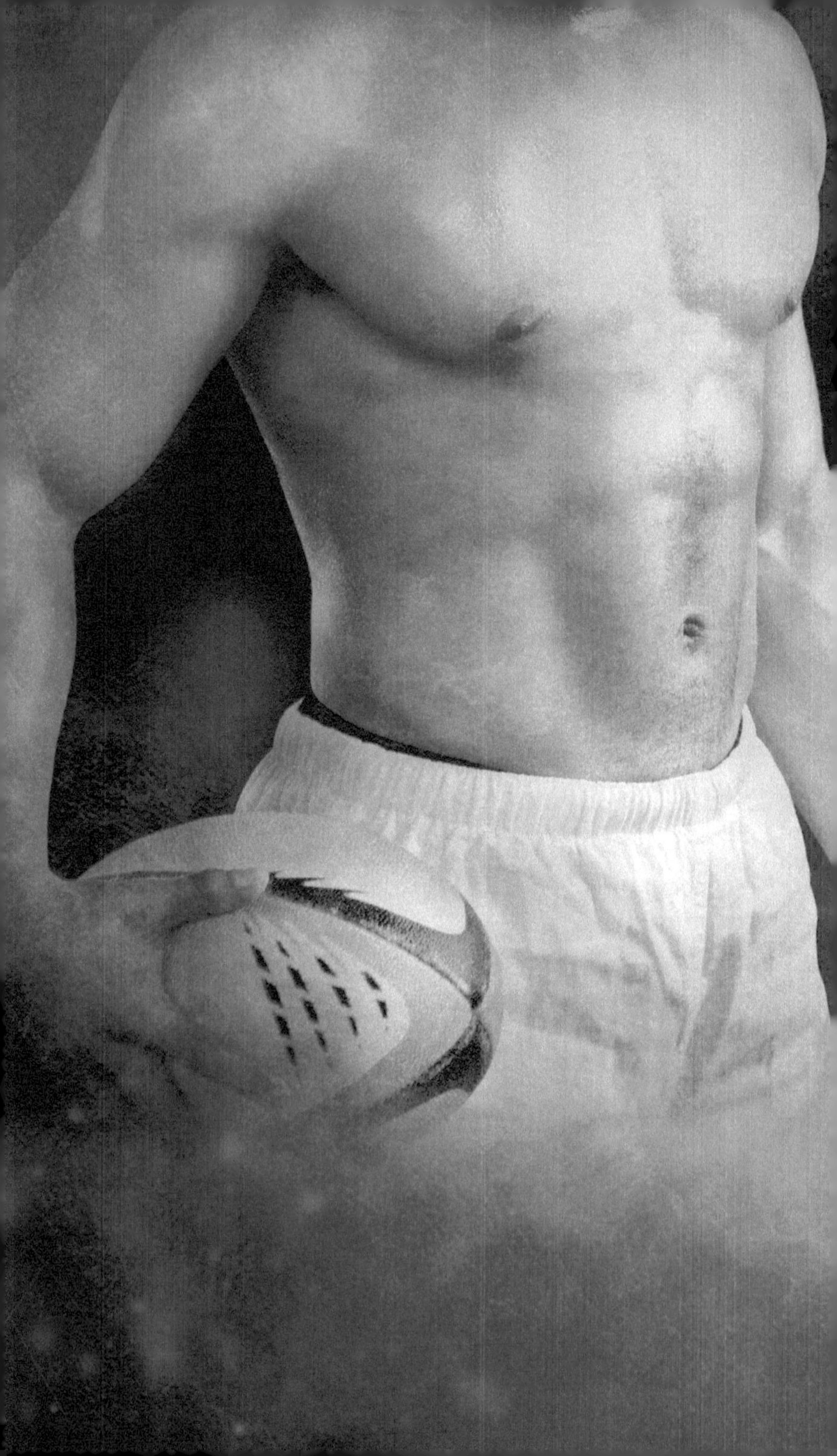

Chapter Sixteen

Chelsea

"You good?" Dallas pulled a chair out and lowered himself into it. The feet scraped on the tiled floor as he dragged it back to the table. His hand was immediately on my thigh, fingers gripping firmly, but out of sight of anyone else in the cafeteria. "You look ready to stab some asshole."

"I'm all right," I said before he could offer to do it for me. "I have a lot on my mind."

He slipped his hand up a little higher. "Happy to help you forget, but you look like you need to get it off your chest, not get off. Who fucked with you? Apart from...you know." He managed a half smile.

I managed one myself, but it was watery at best. "I can't say anyone in particular did. There's a lot going on, you know?"

His brows knitted. "I feel like I'm missing something important here."

He was, but I hadn't found an opportunity to explain that to him yet. I would, but the right place wasn't here, in front of a room full of people. I could fill him in on the other thing that was on my mind.

"Doctor Stuart gave his recommendation to the GM that he hire me," I said.

"Okay," Dallas said slowly. "That's good, right?"

"It's very good," I agreed.

"You still look like someone kicked your puppy." He ran his thumb over the top of my thigh.

"I'm worried he'll hire someone else," I admitted. "I've considered what I'll do if I don't get to work here, but not seriously. Maybe I should have." I shrugged. "There's no guarantees."

"We could go on strike," he offered. "I'll tell the GM we won't play unless he hires you." He looked ready to stand up right now and stomp off to Bruce Fergus' office to set him straight.

"Please don't do that," I said quickly. "I want to be hired because I'm the right person for the job. Not because you guys blackmailed him into it." I made a mental note to tell my brother not to blackmail the GM either. That was something he'd do, under the misguided belief it would make me happy. Okay, maybe not so misguided, but I still didn't want him doing it. I had to stand on my own two feet.

Dallas sagged slightly. "Okay, I won't if you don't want me to. But I'm not taking it off the table completely. If that's what I have to do to keep you around, then I will."

"It wouldn't hurt you if I worked somewhere else," I said. It might even be for the best.

He leaned in and lowered his voice. "It would hurt my cock. If my balls had hearts, they'd break. Right now, I'm resisting the urge to fuck you right here on the top of the table." He looked pained. "I'm addicted and I don't want help. I need to be inside you all the time."

"If it's distracting you from playing..." I started.

"It's not," he said hurriedly. "That's the only time I can think about anything else. The moment training is over, or the game ends, you're in my head. Move in with me."

I blinked in surprise. Storm had tried to insist I live with him, but I'd put him off for now. Dallas hadn't mentioned it before this, nor had Frost.

"I don't know if that's a good idea," I said slowly.

"It is," he stated. "We'll come to work together. We'll spend all night with my cock in your pussy.

Every night." His hazel eyes were wild with the possibilities.

"Until I know where I'm going to work, everything is up in the air," I said. "And we have to consider the other guys. And there's a few things you don't know about me that could change your mind."

"There's nothing you could say that would change my mind about you," he insisted. "I love you. I need you." He looked like a man who'd been lost in the desert for a week, searching for water.

"When you're finished for the day, come and find me," I said. "There are things I need to show you. If you don't hate me afterwards, we can think about it."

I didn't miss him telling me he loved me. I cared about him, but once he knew the truth, he might run faster than he did when he had possession of the ball. He might look at me the way he had the first time he fucked me. When he realised what I was and that Storm paid me to be with him, he called me a whore before bolting from the room.

He might call me worse than that this time.

"I'll find you and come," he said. "If I can hold out that long." He pressed his lips together like he was in pain.

I never had any man react to me the way he did. Lover or client, none had literally not been able to get enough of me. At times, I wondered if he had any skin left on his cock. Or how I had any skin left on the inside of my pussy. When he fucked me, he was rarely slow and gentle. Especially if it was a couple of days between fucks, then he was frantic and rough, desperate to get his fix.

I loved every moment of it.

I glanced down at my watch. "I have about ten minutes before I have to—"

Dallas shot to his feet. "Where?" His eyes were wild again. Dark with need. "I know a place." He seemed ready to throw me over his shoulder and carry me there, but he waited for me to grab my phone and follow him out of the cafeteria.

I didn't dare to look back to see if anyone was watching. Hopefully they'd only interpret it as a doctor seeing her client during her lunch break. That wasn't far off. He'd likely insist if he didn't fuck me in the next couple of minutes he'd lose his mind.

He led me to the equipment room, which was empty at this time of day. Off to the side, was another door with the words 'cleaning supplies' written on the front.

He wrenched the door open and pressed me inside before closing it behind us. It barely clicked shut before he had me pinned to the wall. He rucked up the front of my skirt, shoved my panties aside and pushed two fingers straight into my pussy.

"You're so wet." He pushed down the front of his track pants freeing his cock. Pulling his fingers out of me, he pulled up one of my legs and positioned his cock before slamming right inside me. "Fuck, yes. This."

He pulled all the way out before ramming back into me. Over and over he thrust, his breathing ragged like a wild animal in heat. Holding me in place with one hand, he slid the other between us to circle my clit with his fingers.

"I'm giving up football," he panted. "I'm going to keep you at home with me and fuck you all day long. And all night."

I managed a small, breathless laugh. "You're not giving up football. And we both need sleep once in a while."

"Fuck sleep," he growled. "I just want to fuck you. You're a witch, you put me under some kind of spell. If there's an antidote, I won't take it. I'll keep taking *you*."

"Not a witch," I said. He drove me closer and closer to the edge, making it more difficult to think. He might not be the only one with a problem. I couldn't get enough of him or the other guys. The more time I spent with them, the more orgasms they gave me, the more I wanted. The more I needed.

"Dallas," I whispered. "I'm going to come."

"Come," he said. "Come on my cock. Then I'm going to come inside you. You're going to take every drop, because you're mine. Mine. And I'm yours."

For half a second, I remembered it might be the last time he said that to me, but I was washed away with the intensity of an orgasm that exploded around me like the end of the universe and the beginning of another one. I shattered into a million stars before coming back together again.

He followed close behind, pumping into me, biting back a grunt and a growl. He ground against me, milking himself, trying to draw out his orgasm as long as possible. Filling me up to the brim with his release.

He sagged against the wall, puffing, his chest hard against mine. "Fuck. I didn't want that to end. You're so fucking perfect. So fucking *mine*."

"You're so fucking gorgeous and so fucking mine," I said. I'd make him understand somehow. I wasn't going to let him run away from me or the other guys. I didn't know how, but I would. Whatever it took, I wasn't ready to lose him.

"So fucking yours," he agreed. "Storm is going to be disappointed. He didn't get to watch."

I laughed, low and husky from the back of my throat. "He can watch next time."

"Can I ask you something?" He buried his face in my hair.

"How can I say no to a guy when his cock is still deep inside me?" I asked.

He gave it a wiggle, making me laugh again. "Have you fucked Atlas?"

"No, I haven't," I said carefully. I hadn't had much chance to be alone with him since our date. Between his schedule and mine, we were both busy. I made a mental note to rectify that. If he wanted to. He didn't seem intimidated by the other guys, but the situation was complicated. If he wanted to back away from it, I wouldn't blame him. But I would be disappointed.

"When you do, can I watch?" Dallas asked softly. "I know the others don't like him, but I don't think he's the asshole they think he is."

"He really isn't," I agreed. "If he doesn't mind you watching, then I don't." Now I was picturing exactly that. Atlas lying on top of me, thrusting into me while Dallas sat beside us, his gaze on us both. I had a sneaking suspicion Atlas would be as into that as we were.

A shiver of anticipation passed through me. These guys opened doors to opportunities I hadn't even dreamt of. I couldn't wait to experience every one of them. I'd had a lot of sex, but I felt as though I hadn't begun to experience it.

It was my turn to ask, "Can I ask you a question?"

"Anything," he said without hesitation.

"Do you just want to watch, or do you want to... take part? With him." In my mind, the grunts and groans I heard out on the field became the sound of them straining as they fucked each other. The visual image was almost enough to make me come again.

Dallas swallowed audibly. "I don't know. Maybe."

"What about Jay?" I only met him in passing, but as far as I could tell, Jay and Atlas were tight. Ramsey too, but I didn't know where he fit into the picture.

"I don't know," Dallas said again. "As long as I have you, then I can roll with anything else. You're my woman and I'm not letting you go. Ever. That whole CNC thing was everything. Everything I do with you is... Everything." He pressed his forehead against mine.

"So are you," I whispered. I could definitely see myself falling head over heels for him.

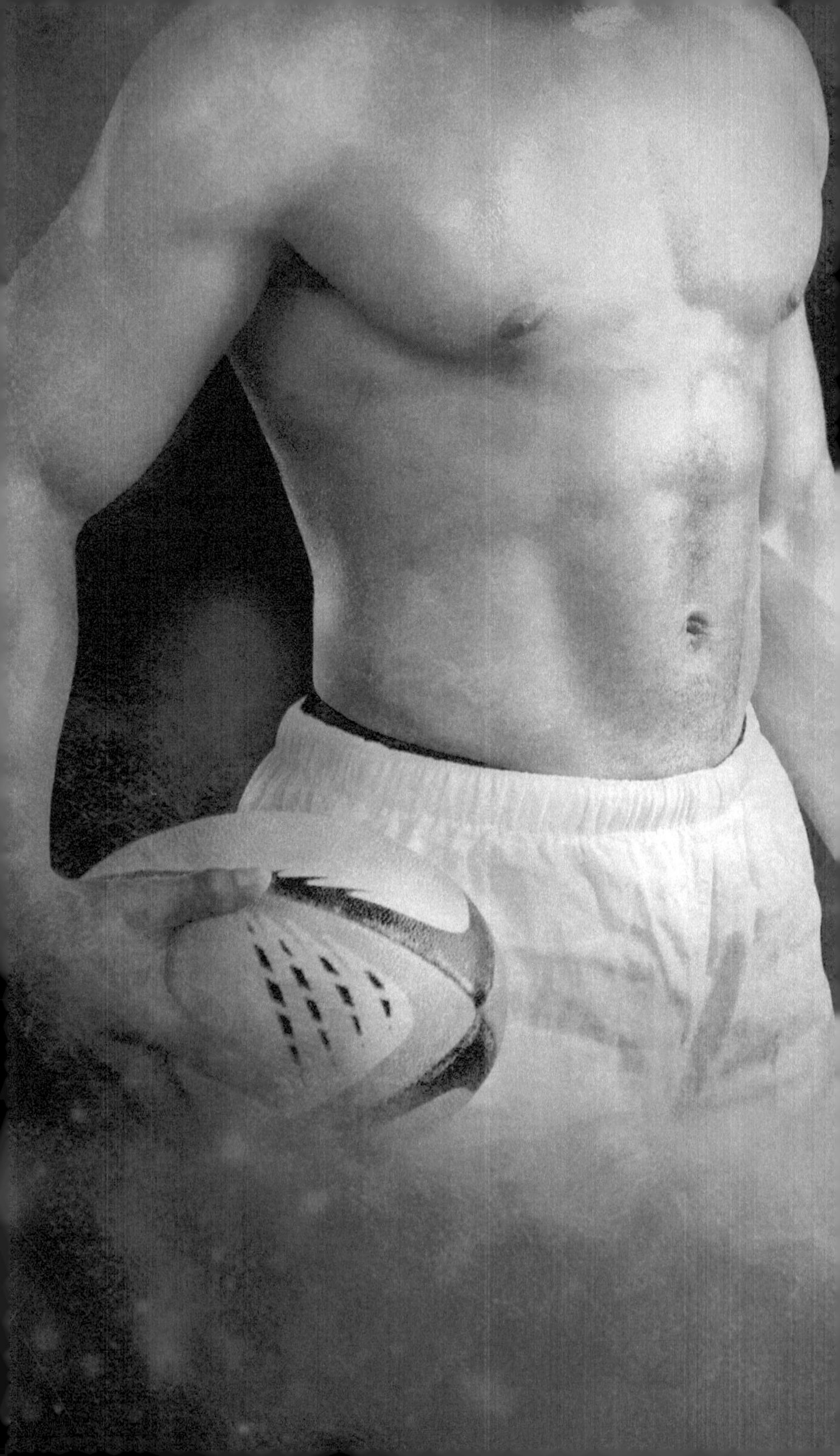

Chapter Seventeen

Frost

"Where are we going?" I caught up with Chelsea and Dallas before they could get into her car. He looked like his usual, sullen self, but she looked pensive. It wasn't difficult to figure out why. Because of that, I decided to invite myself along.

I sensed another presence behind me before Storm spoke.

"Same question." He stood beside me and rested his elbow on my shoulder like he was pretending to be casual. From a distance, it would look like we were having a pleasant chat. Close up, none of us were fooled. The air was laced with tension.

Chelsea glanced over at us, some of the tension leaving her body. She jangled the keys in her hand.

"We're going on a field trip. You boys want to tag along?"

"If we're not intruding," I said at the same time as Storm said, "Yes."

Dallas looked like he thought we were very much intruding.

Before he could say anything, Chelsea put her hand on his arm.

"They should come too. This involves all of us." She caught my eye and gave me a slight nod.

I half wanted to turn and walk away right now, but curiosity and the fact these people were my family, forced my feet forward to climb into the back of the car.

Storm looked annoyed at having to sit in the back, but he got as close to me as possible. "You sure about this?" he said in my ear.

"More than I should be," I replied.

I wasn't exactly sure where Chelsea was taking us, but I made a few educated guesses. I sat back to enjoy the ride, grooving along to Ice Blue Roses playing through the car speakers. "I love this song."

"You act like we're going on a road trip," Storm said.

I grinned. "Aren't we? We have a car, us and

good music. What more could anyone want?" I knew what I wanted, but I didn't dare to hope. That might be too much when it came to introducing Dallas to the real Dusk Bay. I was still slightly horrified at myself, but I was ready to embrace that part of me. As long as I stayed within the right boundaries, I could feed my darkest needs. And do it with a smile.

"At least she didn't invite Atlas," he grumbled.

"He might be meeting us there," I said lightly. I couldn't help trying to stir him up a little bit. He knew as well as I did that if Chelsea wanted to get involved with him too, that's what would happen. None of us would try to stop it.

Storm grunted. He muttered something that sounded like 'asshole,' but it didn't seem to be directed at me.

I had an idea of how to bring the two together, but that would have to wait until after this. I made a note to speak to Chelsea about it. Although, I had no doubt she'd agree. The better we all got along with each other, the better it was for her. We'd all do anything for her, so why not stop hating on Atlas?

Chelsea pulled the car up in front of a nondescript building on the edge of Dusk Bay. The façade was dark, almost oppressive, like a modern Gothic building.

"What is this place?" Dallas asked.

"You'll see," Chelsea said. She shot us all a dazzling smile before climbing out of the car and heading towards the front door of the building.

I exchanged confused looks with Storm, but hurried to follow her.

We caught up with her as a man in a dark suit opened the door and looked appraisingly at all four of us. His gaze lingered on Chelsea, but the air of danger around him suggested it was better to let it go. This time.

This wasn't someone I could strangle and leave for someone else to deal with. I suspected if I tried anything, I'd be the one lying dead. I couldn't see a weapon, but I was almost certain he had one.

"Welcome, Miss Miller," he finally said. He stood aside and nodded for us to enter.

I hesitated, but Chelsea lifted her chin and stepped inside like she owned the place. If she thought it was safe to enter, I guessed it was. Hoped it was.

We walked down a short corridor and into an opulent room that made my jaw drop.

The walls and leather furniture were black, as were the sleek tables that took up much of the space. Gold light fittings hung from the ceiling, dripping with crystals. Even the floors, a dark hardwood, looked expensive.

Those weren't even the most expensive looking things in the room. Several men and women sat around the tables. Their clothes alone would have fed a small country for a year. In track pants and a Smashers hoodie, I felt underdressed.

"I think we just stepped into the nineteen twenties," Storm said.

"Chelsea!" A dark-haired woman a handful of years older than her hopped up from a chair and hurried over to give Chelsea a hug. "I haven't seen you in ages."

"Daze!" Chelsea hugged her back. "I was hoping you'd be here."

"Where else would I be on a Tuesday?" Daze asked. "Mina is here too. Come and sit with us." She glanced appraisingly at us.

"Guys, this is Daisy LaSalle," Chelsea introduced. "Daze, this is Storm Keller, Dallas Gregory and Daniel Frost."

"My friends call me Frost." I offered Daze my hand.

She eyed it for a moment before she shook it. "It's nice to meet you, Frost. And you too," she said to the other guys. She hooked her arm through Chelsea's and led her over to a table. "What brings all of you here today?"

A dainty, dark-haired woman sat at a table in the corner, a dark-haired man beside her. He had a similar air to Ice, and the man at the door. A smile hovered around the corners of his lips, but he looked like he could pull out a knife and slash open a throat without blinking.

"Gianni." He leaned over the table to shake my hand. "This is Mina."

Mina nodded, but kept her hands in her lap. She gave me the impression she was watching everything and absorbing it for future reference. If I was going to be intimidated by anyone in this room, it would be her.

Ironic, given she was at least half my size. I'd lived long enough to know not to underestimate a woman. And in this place? Even more so.

"Storm and Frost have recently been introduced to the real Dusk Bay," Chelsea was saying as she slid into a chair beside Daze. "I thought this would be a good way to show Dallas."

Dallas sat on the other side of Chelsea and looked confused. His eyes kept darting from her, to me, to the other people around the table and back to her. "Rich people in some kind of secret club?"

"It's an exclusive club," Gianni said. "This is where people come to make deals. And they make a fabulous martini." He nodded towards the drink on the table in front of him.

"What kind of deals?" Storm asked.

"All kinds," Gianni said. "Some of them are even legal."

"We didn't just step back into the nineteen twenties," I said. "We stepped into a speakeasy, like in the mafia movies."

"Not just movies." Gianni picked up his drink, toasted me and took a sip.

Dallas frowned. "What the fuck?" He stared at Chelsea, the cogs and wheels almost visibly turning in his mind. "Are you saying this is some kind of mafia place?"

"Basically," she said simply. "The people in this room run Dusk Bay."

"We run the country," Mina said quietly. "Most of it anyway."

"Holy shit," I whispered. This went way beyond strangling one woman.

I'd had a sense of *something* the moment I walked in the room. Now I knew what it was. It was a hum of power. It drew me like a magnet. Grabbed me in a stranglehold and held me with possibilities I never considered before.

"Are we a part of that now?"

"What the hell are you talking about?" Dallas demanded. "You're some kind of mafia princess?" His hazel eyes were wide. He only blinked every once in a while, trying to get his head around what he was hearing.

"I wouldn't exactly describe myself that way, but yes," Chelsea said.

"Me too," Daze said with a smile. "Mina is more like a mafia queen. One of her boyfriends is the head of all of this." She gestured around the room.

Mina inclined her head.

"That makes me a queen too," Gianni said cheerfully. "Or a king. I'll happily own both of those."

"I don't—" Dallas shook his head. "The mafia are criminals. They launder money, bribe people, threaten and all that shit."

"Give the boy a gold star," Gianni said. "We do all of those things and a lot more. In return, we get to live like this." He raised his drink again, his tattooed fingers curled around the base of the glass.

"Sign me the fuck up," I said softly. I was already in this up to my eyeballs, but the more they talked about it, the more involved I wanted to be. How far could this go? I had no illusions about becoming a mob boss, but the connections I could make would be a game changer.

I glanced over at Storm. He looked thoughtful, maybe resistant, but he nodded.

"Me too," he said finally. His gaze held caution, but he wasn't going to be left behind. Knowing him, he was already trying to figure out how to elbow people like Gianni out of the way. Fortunately, I knew he wouldn't be rash and get himself killed. At least, I hoped he wouldn't. That would suck.

All of our eyes turned to Dallas.

His attention was on Chelsea. "You're okay with this?"

"It doesn't matter whether I am or whether I'm not," she said. "This is the reality of Dusk Bay." One she'd clearly had a long time to get used to. One that seemed intent on sucking her back in, even though she didn't want to get involved.

Dallas glanced over to me and Storm. "You knew?"

"Only recently," I said. "We agreed you should know as soon as possible."

"Right." He frowned and turned back to Chelsea. "Whatever you're into, I'm into. Even if it is as fucked up as it sounds." He wasn't completely convinced, but it didn't matter. If the option was walking away from her, he'd stick around and let her drag him into anything. That look in his eyes wasn't just obsession. He was head over heels in love with her. She could have asked him to walk into the ocean and he would have. He was absolutely gone.

"He says fucked up like it's a bad thing," Gianni remarked.

Daze grinned. "It takes some getting used to, but we could always use three more big, muscly guys like you. Right, Mina?"

"Possibly," she said. "Only if they're an asset."

"You sound like Caleb," Daze teased.

Whoever Caleb was, Mina looked unimpressed at the comparison.

Daze was completely undeterred. "Are there any more like these three?"

"You have three boyfriends already," Chelsea said flatly.

Daze snorted. "I don't need any more boyfriends. Rugby players are known for being smart as well as muscular. That's a good combination when it comes to our operations."

"That's accurate," Storm said. "We're both."

Grudgingly he added, "Some of the other guys on the team are too."

"I know they are," Daze said. "Some of them already work for us."

I almost choked on air. "They do?"

She turned to me and smiled. "Absolutely."

I gaped at her when she started to name names.

Chapter Eighteen

Chelsea

I SHOULD ABSOLUTELY NOT HAVE BEEN surprised by any of it.

Okay, I wasn't too surprised by how quickly Frost and Storm threw their hats into the proverbial ring. I wasn't even surprised Dallas went along without a fight. I certainly shouldn't have been surprised when Daze started giving the names of members of the team. Of course some of them would have been recruited already.

The guys were more shocked than I was, but it didn't last for long. Like everything else, they took the ball and ran with it.

It wasn't discussed, but I was sure they all knew if they rejected anything they heard, they risked not walking out of there alive. That was why Daze,

Gianni and Mina were so forthcoming. If the guys tried to betray them, they'd have them killed. It was that simple. Until they proved themselves, they'd be watched closely. By me and by members of the team.

Specifically, Atlas Underwood, whose gaze was on them when I stepped into the locker room.

I made my way over to him, moving through the throng of half naked men, while try not to trip over footy boots that lay on the floor.

I peered over his shoulder. "Do you have a minute?"

"I was wondering when you'd come and find me." He didn't take his eyes off Storm, Frost and Dallas. The three of them sat in the corner, talking in low voices. "I understand we have some mutual acquaintances."

"That's my understanding too," I agreed. "Did you know?"

He turned his head slightly. "I suspected. There's a resemblance to your brother, plus you have the same surname."

"Miller is a common name," I pointed out. "Any resemblance might be a coincidence."

"It isn't," he said. Now he turned to look at me. "Your eyes are almost exactly the same colour. Your hair too."

"How long have you suspected?" I asked.

He shrugged. "As soon as I heard your name. Miller might be common, but Dusk Bay is a small place. It was a reasonable assumption."

"So that date—"

He took a couple of steps forward, forcing me to step back until I was pressed against one of the lockers. He was close enough to breathe in my exhalation.

"That was real. Nothing to do with who you're related to. I wanted to get to know you. I still do." His firm chest was pressed against mine, hard muscle robbing me of breath and making it harder to think.

"I know you feel the same way. Is your heart racing as fast as mine?" He raised two fingers and pressed them against the pulse point in my neck. "Faster." In a whisper he added, "How wet are you?"

Before I could answer, he stepped back. Out of reach of Storm, who was about to lunge at him.

"What do you think you're fucking doing?" Storm growled.

Frost and Dallas were right behind him, both looking cautious.

"What does it fucking look like?" Atlas sneered.

"It looks like you're trying to make the moves on my woman," Storm snarled.

Atlas started to clap slowly, sarcastically. "You might not be as dumb as you look." He ducked when Storm took a swing at him. The fullback's fist narrowly missed hitting me right in the face.

I let out a squeak and ducked.

"What the fuck, Storm?" Frost grabbed his arm before he could swing again. "You could have hit her."

Storm shook him off and dropped his hands to his sides. "I wasn't aiming for you." He looked furious with himself.

After a moment, I straightened up. "I knew you weren't. Maybe you could *not* aim at each other either."

"I saw the way he was touching you." Storm scowled at Atlas.

"She wasn't objecting." Atlas smirked. "Could it be that she wants me?"

"I know she fucking does," Storm snapped. "What I don't know is why." His gaze cut to me, questioning.

"I like Atlas," I said. "I like all of you. Would it hurt you to get along?"

"It wouldn't hurt me," Dallas said.

"Me either," Frost agreed.

Storm glared at them both like they were betraying him in some way.

"Why don't you all just compare cock size?" Jay called out from where he stood in front of his locker.

"Because Storm knows he'll lose," Atlas called back.

"Fuck off," Storm growled. He sucked in a harsh breath and let it out through his nose. "You two spend a lot of time thinking about my cock."

"I know I do," Frost said, clearly trying to defuse the situation.

"Me too," I agreed. "I spend a lot of time thinking about all of the cocks."

"All of them?" Atlas looked smug.

I shrugged. "I like cock." I wasn't ashamed of it. I had no intention of ever being ashamed.

"You'll love mine," Atlas said. "I know what to do with it."

Dallas and Frost both grabbed Storm before he could lunge at Atlas again.

"Someone needs to wipe that look off the prick's face." Storm struggled against them.

Frost let go of Storm's arm, ducked under and grabbed a fist full of Atlas' shirt.

I thought he was going to punch the other player, but instead he smashed his mouth against his.

Atlas froze for a second or two, then he kissed Frost back. Only for a handful of seconds before he pulled away, gaping.

He glanced over to Jay who stood staring, uncomprehending. That expression quickly turned to anger before Jay grabbed up his duffel bag and stomped out of the locker room.

"Jay!" Atlas pushed away from Frost and ran after him until they both disappeared out the door.

"He doesn't look so smug now," Storm remarked.

I rubbed my temples and closed my eyes for a few moments. "I thought you were going to try to get along with each other."

"I was," Frost said. He looked like he couldn't believe what he'd done. At the same time, he clearly didn't regret it. "I thought that was better than punching the shit out of him."

"I think he preferred it," I said.

At least in the moment. Before he saw the hurt on Jay's face. That confirmed what I already suspected. Did it go both ways though? Jay clearly cared about Atlas as more than a friend, but I wasn't sure how Atlas felt.

If I could, I'd pin him down and figure a few things out. Or let him pin me down.

Either worked for me. The way he had me

pressed against the locker, his warm fingers on my neck, I was so ready for more. I wouldn't have stopped him if he'd fucked me then and there. If it wasn't for Storm, and the potential of raising eyebrows with the team, he might have.

"I know I did," Frost said. "He's a good kisser."

Storm growled.

Frost gave him a sideways hug and pressed his lips to the fullback's cheek. "Not as good as you."

"Better not be," Storm said.

Dallas was staring at them both. "Why do you always have to make trouble? You in particular, Storm. Did you see Chelsea objecting to Atlas touching her? Do you think she's not capable of pushing him away if that's what she wants? Because she is. But you have to stomp over there and make a big fucking deal out of it."

"It is a big fucking deal," Storm said. "He was touching her."

"Because. She. Wanted. Him. To." Dallas glared at him. "She's made her thoughts on the subject clear. Have some fucking respect."

Storm leaned back, stared at him, then at me. "I wasn't trying to—" He shook his head. "You know how this works. No one touches her without my permission. No one. I haven't given that to Atlas yet. He's going to have to fucking earn it the way you both did. Other-wise, he can stay the hell away from her." His jaw was set, just like his mind. He wasn't budging a hair on this.

"She gives him her permission," Dallas argued.

"I don't care." Storm's jaw worked as his irritation grew. "He needs my permission too. This woman is fucking mine. I decide who touches her. End of story." He made a slashing gesture through the air with his hand.

Dallas opened his mouth to say more, but I placed a hand on his bicep. "It's okay. Let's not have any more conflict."

I didn't need Storm's permission to decide who touched me and who didn't, but it would be easier if they were all in agreement. This fighting, it was getting none of them anywhere. Instead, it was putting a wedge between them. One that didn't need to be there.

Dallas screwed his eyes shut, and nodded. "Fine, I'll back off. For you. But he needs to back the fuck off too." He sighed out his nose before turning and walking back to his locker.

I watched him leave. If they were going to fight like this, we were going to have problems. Lots of them. This wasn't how I wanted bruises to happen.

"Chelsea—" Frost started.

I opened my eyes when he cupped my cheek with his hand. "I'm okay," I said.

"Are you?" he pressed. "I know you like all of us, and this fighting is a pain in the ass. You're not going to walk away from us, are you?" He elbowed Storm back when the fullback stepped forward, trying to protest.

"I don't want to," I said. "But if this starts to affect the performance of the team, then…"

I couldn't, in good conscience, let the Smashers or their fans suffer because of me. I'd sooner walk away from all of them than have them lose because they were divided over me.

Doing it would break my heart into a million tiny pieces. In the time I'd known them, I'd become very attached to all of them. I couldn't imagine my life without them.

"It won't," Storm insisted.

"I'd sooner give up the team than give you up." Frost's tone matched the soft look in his eyes. "You're more important to me than footy. You both are." He glanced back at Storm.

"I don't want you to give up anything," I said. "I know we can all work together, if we try."

"I'm trying," Frost said. He turned his face to give the fullback an accusing glance.

"I'll try if Atlas respects my boundaries." Storm wasn't giving up any ground. "I don't want some random guy thinking he can touch her."

"Atlas isn't some random guy," Frost argued. "He's our teammate. You agreed to give him a chance, you need to do that."

"Or else what?" Storm's jaw worked harder than ever. "Are you going to run off with him? I haven't forgotten he fucking touched you too." His face was pink with frustration. All the way up to the tips of his ears. Any other time, it would have been adorable. Right then, he was a firecracker waiting for an open flame.

"*I* touched *him*," Frost reminded him. "I'm not going to run off with anyone except you two, but if you keep pushing people away, you might find yourself alone." He turned his back on Storm.

Storm glared at him for a few moments, before stomping away to his locker.

"I'm sorry. He can be intense. I think, deep down he's scared of losing us," Frost whispered.

"I don't think it's that deep down," I said.

I remembered what Storm told me about his family. He lost people he cared about before. He was terrified it would happen again. That fear manifested itself in anger. Getting angry with the wrong people in Dusk Bay could get you killed. We'd have to find a way to make him feel secure before the shit hit the fan.

My phone vibrated in my pocket. I pulled it out and glanced at the screen.

Swallowed hard.

"I need to go."

Chapter Nineteen

Chelsea

Nerves fluttering in my chest, I approached the general manager's office. His personal assistant sat at the desk in front of his doorway.

"Mr Fergus asked to see me," I said.

"Of course." She smiled warmly. I bet she did to everyone. Even those about to be fired. "Go right on in, he's expecting you." She jerked her head in the direction of the ajar door.

"Thank you." I stepped over and knocked before placing my palm on the door and pushing it open further.

The GM sat beside his desk, his phone to his ear. He waved for me to come inside and sit in the seat opposite him.

"I totally agree," he said to whoever he was talking to. "That wasn't something we expected... I realise that, but we'll be better prepared the next time." He was silent for a moment before chuckling. "There's always a next time. None of us are in any doubt... Exactly." He chuckled again. "Okay, I have to go. Tell Bob to pull his head in. Yeah, you too."

He ended the call and placed the phone down on his desk.

"You wanted to see me?" I said, trying like hell to keep my nerves from showing.

Bruce Fergus was in his fifties, his hair streaked with grey, particularly around his temples. He was an undeniably attractive man who used to play rugby himself. As far as I could tell, he seemed committed to the sport in general, and the Smashers in particular. The guys respected him, which might be the only thing they all had in common.

"Yes, I did," he said. He leaned forward, his elbows on the top of the desk. "Doctor Stuart speaks highly of you. It's his opinion that I owe you an interview for a position with the team."

"I'm sure you don't owe me anything," I said carefully. "But I'd appreciate the opportunity."

He sat back and crossed his arms. "That's true, I don't, but I respect the opinion of Doctor Stuart.

What do you think you can bring to the team that another doctor can't, Doctor Miller?"

Apparently we were going straight into interview mode. I would have liked time to prepare, but this was my chance to demonstrate my ability to think on my feet.

"Commitment," I said firmly. "I understand the ins and outs of the team and what the job entails. I'm ready to be on call all day, every day, and all night. I'm ready to undertake any and all training to increase my knowledge and qualifications."

"Hmmm, that's a very 'interview candidate' answer," Bruce said. "What do you, as a person, hope to give to the team?"

"If you don't mind me being honest, sir, I love the Smashers. I love everything about them. I love the game, I love their commitment to it. I love Dusk Bay. The first time I ever saw a game of rugby, I knew what I wanted to do with my life. This is it. Working with this team."

"And if you don't get that opportunity?" His expression gave away nothing.

"Then I'll work somewhere else and wait for another position to open up," I said. "And I'll apply again and again until you hire me."

"And if I never do?" he shot back.

"You have to retire eventually," I said, not blinking.

He chuckled. "That's true. I admire your tenacity."

"It's taken me this far," I said. "This practical placement has been incredible. For me, it's confirmed this is what I'm meant to be doing. From the moment I walked through the door, I felt like I belonged here."

"This place has a way of doing that to you." He seemed to be thinking back to the first time he stepped foot in the stadium.

"It does," I agreed. "If you don't mind me saying, I think the team deserves people who are ready and willing to give them their all."

"And you think that's you?" he asked.

"Yes, I do," I said. "One hundred percent." I paused for a moment. "No, I don't think it's me, I *know* it's me." Storm's cockiness must be rubbing off on me. Did Bruce know about my relationship with the guys?

He'd be one hell of a poker player, because I had no idea what he was thinking. He could be humouring me, and he could be genuinely interested in what I had to say. Either way, it was making me increasingly nervous.

"No wonder Doctor Stuart likes you," Bruce said. He didn't elaborate on that. "You have final exams to sit?"

"Next week," I said. "After that, I'll be ready. I can start full-time on Monday week."

"You don't want a break before jumping into working full-time?" he asked.

"The season starts right after," I said. "I accelerated my degree to do this final component over the Christmas trimester. I wanted to time it so I was ready in time."

"That's some foresight," he said.

"When you want something, you have to do what you have to do to make it happen," I said. "I'm sure you know that. Having played rugby at a professional level, you would have made sacrifices to get there. It would have been worth it when you made the winning try in the grand final and held up that cup. Before doing a shoey."

I'd taken the time to research him, including watching a video of him drinking champagne out of his football boot. A strange, but proud Australian tradition.

He chuckled again. "Best moment of my life. The win, not so much the shoey. That tasted as good as it sounds." He grimaced, but his face relaxed into a smile.

I grinned. "I bet it did." It must have been full of all sorts of sweat and germs. As long as no one asked me to do it, I wouldn't judge them too harshly.

"Maybe we should make that a requirement of all our employees," he mused out loud. "One shoey each."

"I have a funny feeling there are laws against making staff do that," I said lightly. "But if it's a team spirit thing, you might get a few takers."

"But not you?" he asked.

In my life, I'd had a variety of things in my mouth, but I still wasn't interested in this. I held up my foot so he could see my leather sandals. "I don't think they'd survive the experience, even if they'd hold liquid."

"Point taken." He lowered his arms and sat forward again. "How would you describe yourself, Doctor Miller?"

"Firstly, I'd suggest you call me Chelsea," I said. "I'm not big on formality. Sir."

He gestured for me to continue.

"I'd describe myself as driven," I said slowly. "Committed. Dedicated. I tend to jump into things with both feet and throw everything into it. Every-thing I do, I give it all I have."

"That seems to be a personality trait for doctors," he said. "What makes you different from the others?"

The others aren't fucking half the team, I thought.

At least, as far as I knew, they weren't. Admittedly, I wasn't privy to what the other players did in their spare time, much less any other candidates for this job. They could be banging like rabbits for all I knew.

"I'm not looking at this opportunity as a stepping stone," I continued. "I'm not looking to work here then eventually move to one of the teams in Europe. My goal is to take over for Doctor Stuart some day. I know some people would say that's shortsighted. That I lack ambition. I disagree. Working for the Smashers would be a privilege. One I'd wholeheartedly embrace. I believe continuity of care is important, and that goes beyond the players' current situation. If they move into coaching, management or move away from the game entirely, they could look forward to knowing someone is watching out for all their medical needs."

"If one of those teams from Europe was to offer you a substantial pay raise to move there, what would you do?" he asked.

"I'd be lying if I said I wouldn't consider it," I said. "I mean, you did say *substantial*. At the end of the day, I don't see myself working anywhere but here. It's about more than money, you know? I think it's important for people to love what they do, and I've loved every moment of being here. It's not just a job for me. It's a passion."

"I can see that," he said approvingly. "What are you going to do if you end up working with someone who doesn't agree with you? Someone whom, for whatever reason, you don't get along with?"

That was a loaded question. Did he know about Storm and Atlas not getting along? Locker room disagreements were nothing new in any sport, much less this one.

I decided it was a generic question and cleared my throat to respond.

"I'll continue to do my job," I said. "We can't always like who we work with." Now I was thinking about Ivy and her snarky comments. I regretted her death, even though there was nothing I could have done to change what happened. If we'd been friends, she might still have ended up with Frost's hands wrapped around her throat. She would have been just as dead.

"As long as everyone can be respectful, I don't see why it needs to impact our work, or the team."

"What if they're not respectful?" he asked. "What if they're just those people who refuse to go along with you, and insist on doing things their way?"

"Then I'll look at their way and see if it's better," I said. "It might be a good opportunity for me to learn a different way of doing things."

"And if it isn't?" he asked. "If you can't resolve your differences and work together, then what will you do?"

"Then I follow team protocol," I said. "I'm sure there are processes for people to come together to find middle-ground. But that would be a last resort."

"Why is that?" he asked. "Why not do what you can to clear up any problems before they become bigger problems?"

Because snitches get stitches? I thought.

"Because I suspect you have better things to do than mediate between two responsible adults," I said. "Anyone who works here should have the same agenda: what's best for the team. As long as we both want that, there's no reason we can't find common ground."

He nodded. He seemed to like that answer. Or at

least, he wasn't dismissing it out of hand. That had to be a good thing, right? I was sure he wouldn't have preferred I say I'd go running to him every time I had a problem with a co-worker. No boss wanted that, did they? Divina certainly wouldn't. She'd make sure staff didn't work at the same time, if she could. Otherwise, she'd expect them to suck it up and move on.

"All right, Doctor— Chelsea. Thank you very much for coming to see me." He stood and offered me his hand. "I'll be in touch. Or my assistant will."

I shook his hand. I hadn't expected to be hired on the spot, but I had no idea what he was thinking, or if the interview went well. I hadn't done many, so I had nothing to compare it to. I *felt* like I performed well, but I could be completely wrong. Or maybe it went well, and everyone else's went better.

Overthinking for the win.

"Thank you for your time, sir. I appreciate the opportunity, and the interview."

He nodded his dismissal and sank back into his chair. Before he looked back down at his laptop, he said, "Call me Bruce."

"Okay," I said to the top of his head before stepping out of his office and away.

Chapter Twenty

Frost

"What did Bruce say?" I handed Chelsea a bowl of rice, steamed vegetables and chicken. I picked up my own bowl and sat beside Chelsea on her couch. Like always, Dallas sat on the other side of her, his hand on her thigh.

"He asked me a bunch of questions about myself and how I looked at the team," she said.

"Upwards." I spooned chicken into my mouth and smiled while looking up at the ceiling. "Sometimes you're looking down at us too." My gaze shifted to the floor.

She snorted. "That wasn't what he was asking. He wanted to know how committed I was to the Smashers. Stuff like that. Probably the same questions he asked everyone."

"He didn't get inappropriate?" Storm asked darkly.

"Definitely not," she said. "He was very professional."

"He better be." Storm dug into his own bowl of food.

"Or what?" Dallas matched his tone. "You're going to punch him?"

"Yep," Storm said unapologetically. "Or our new connections could deal with him."

"Don't kill the GM," Chelsea said, looking unamused. "And don't have him killed either. Also, it's a good idea not to ask for things of our *connections*, especially things like that. People like Daze and Gianni, they seem nice, but everything they do, they want something in return. Be careful not to end up with a debt you don't want to have to repay."

"What would they want in return?" I asked curiously.

"Nothing is off the table," she said flatly.

My brow dipped. "So, I owe your brother?" I asked. "For helping me with Ivy?"

"I'd say so, yes," she agreed. "He didn't mention that?" She seemed irritated, but I suspected it was directed at Ice, not at me.

"We were kinda busy at the time," I said. "He

suggested he'd guide me, but didn't mention a debt." I wasn't too worried about it. At this point, I didn't think there was too much he could ask that I wasn't happy to try. Unless it meant killing someone in this room, which seemed unlikely.

She sighed. "It'll come."

"Speaking of coming," I said. "You seem tense. Can I give you something to relax you?" I didn't miss the way the other two stiffened, starting with their shoulders and moving down.

Neither said a word of objection. I looked from one to the other. Dallas' eyes were dark already, and Storm had a growing tent in the front of his track pants.

Yeah, I didn't think they'd object.

I looked back to Chelsea and smiled.

"Okay, but give me time to finish my food first," she said.

I didn't think she'd object either. I never met anyone who was open to so much variety. So much experimentation. So much wish fulfilment. It made me love her even more.

"Anyone else down?" I asked with cautious optimism.

"Fuck nope," Dallas grunted. "I'm not interested in being a fuck doll."

I nodded, giving him no judgement whatsoever. What one person was into wasn't always going to be for everyone. "Storm?"

His jaw worked back and forth, giving the suggestion serious consideration. That in itself was interesting. I thought he'd immediately refuse. The man loved nothing more than to be in control. Giving that up, even for a few hours, would be a challenge.

Finally, he said, "No drugs. I'm not going to risk failing a drug test. But we can try stuff."

I mulled that over for a moment before I nodded. "I can roll with that." I finished my dinner and headed back to the kitchen to fill a glass with water. I pulled a small bag out of my pocket and took out a pill. Lucky I thought to put them in there a couple of hours ago. Just in case.

With everyone watching closely, I dropped it into the water and handed it to Chelsea.

She looked me in the eyes and drank down every drop like it was my cum, before handing the glass back.

"You're so hot," I told her. I returned the glass to the kitchen and offered her my hand. I pulled her to her feet and led her to the bedroom.

"Why don't you strip for us before the drug takes

effect?" I sat down on the end of the bed, leaving room for Storm to sit on one side and Dallas on the other.

"I need music," she said.

Dallas pulled out his phone and started to play the first song on his playlist.

We all looked at him.

"What?" He stared back at us. "I like Keith Urban."

"Me too," I said. "But he's not exactly stripping music is he?"

"I can work with it," Chelsea said with a laugh. Like she had back at Flirts, she locked her eyes on us and started to dance, slowly peeling off layers of clothes. Teasing us and moving her body, mesmerising us. Making me hard as steel.

Her movements slowed as the drug began to take effect.

I jumped up and grabbed her before she staggered out of her panties. The other two were right beside me, tearing off the lace and picking her up to lie her back on the bed.

"Now I'm relaxed," she said with a half laugh. "I feel like jelly."

"You look like heaven," I said.

She really did, lying there in the middle of her

pale blue sheets, hair fanned out around her. Her body relaxed, ready for us to do whatever we wanted to her, to use her in any way we liked.

"You look like a fuck doll," Dallas said reverently. He quickly stripped out of his clothes and lay beside her, running his hands up and down her body and between her legs.

"She really does." Storm stripped out of his and lay on the other side of her. If she was a fuck doll, he was a fuck god. His body was toned and hard. Sculpted like he was made from a piece of granite by a master artist.

I couldn't decide which one of them was hotter. I decided it was a tie and shed my own clothes before joining them on the bed.

"I feel like...I shouldn't," Dallas whispered. He still knelt between her legs, lifted her hips with his hands and pressed his cock inside her. "Fuuuck." He closed his eyes, an expression of pure bliss on his face. "She's so..."

"Yeah, she is," I agreed. All of that and more.

The corners of her mouth twitched up in a smile, her eyes half-closed. She was enjoying this as much as Dallas. Completely letting go. Allowing us to fuck her however we wanted to. Giving up all control. It was the hottest thing I ever saw.

That and the way Storm's cock jotted up, pointing towards the ceiling, insisting on being touched.

I was happy to comply. I scooted down the bed and wrapped my fingers around his length. Eyes on his, I teased his cock with the tip of my tongue.

"You want more?" I asked.

"You know I do," he said, his voice rough with need.

"What do you want?" I wasn't sure if he would answer. Talking about sexual needs was as difficult for us as talking about emotions. Maybe more so. Okay, definitely more so.

In the end, I was right, he didn't talk, not with words. He placed his large hand on the back of my head and pushed me further down his cock. Pressing himself inside, all the way to the back of my throat.

I gagged, but I liked it. I wrapped my lips around him as tight as I could and sucked while he thrust slowly, fucking my mouth while Dallas fucked Chelsea.

"Fuck," he groaned. "Wait." He drew himself out of my mouth.

For a moment, I thought he was upset with me. That he might get up and leave. Instead, he gestured for me to turn around, so my cock was in front of his face.

Hell yeah.

His lips and tongue were tentative on me at first, but when I closed my mouth around him again, he followed my lead. Sucking me while I sucked him. Between that and the groans from Dallas, I was hard as hell. And just about to come. So was Storm. I felt it in the tightening of his balls, the way he thrust harder, relentless.

I massaged his hot, firm balls with my hand while lightly grazing my teeth over the sensitive skin that was so fucking hard. So fucking tasty.

He grunted and fell still before coming, squirting salty hot cum into my mouth. It hit the back of my throat and made me gag again. I popped my mouth off him and looked him in the eyes while I swallowed it down. Every last drop.

His eyes widened. He pulled his mouth off me and ran his warm hand up and down my length, pumping me hard until I came on his fingers. The world exploded and all that was left were groans and moans of pleasure. I could have happily stayed in this place forever.

He went on pumping until I finally sagged, panting. Reality, I decided, was better than being in an orgasm bubble. Reality included three of my favourite people in the world. Naked and sweaty. What could be better than that?

I drew in a contented breath, right at the same time Dallas came inside Chelsea. For the first time that night anyway. No doubt, the first of many. He ground into her, eyes closed, spilling his release into her body. Then he too sagged and lay beside her, his cock still inside her as always.

I crawled back up to the top of the mattress, my head beside Storm's.

"That was..." I didn't have words for what it was. Amazing, incredible, awesome. All of those things, but they still weren't enough.

"Yeah," Storm said. That was all I was getting from him tonight. I'd give him time to get his head around it. As much time as he needed. When he was ready, maybe we'd talk about it. Maybe we'd do more. I wouldn't push him. There was no point in doing that, he wouldn't let me anyway. But this? This was a huge step for us. Sharing it with Chelsea made it even more special. Knowing she was watching and enjoying what we were doing with each other. My cock twitched, starting to harden again already. That was what these people did to me. Why I wanted to be around them as much as I could.

No one got me going like they did. No one ever would.

I placed a hand on Storm's bicep, hoping he wouldn't push me away. He didn't. He put a hand over mine and we lay in companionable silence for a while before we got hard again and took turns with Chelsea.

Chapter Twenty One

Chelsea

I woke with Frost's face between my legs. The roofie had worn off, giving me all of my movement back. Every roll of my hips as he ran the tip of his tongue over my slit and swollen clit, he pressed his tongue inside me, thrusting and tasting, moaning in the back of his throat in appreciation.

"You taste so good," he whispered.

I glanced to the side to see Storm and Dallas sitting on the side of the bed, watching. both hard. I lost track of how many times Dallas fucked me, but he was erect now, regardless. Ready.

I turned my face back toward Frost. "You feel so good." He really did have a magical tongue. And fingers. Two of which he pressed into me, while pressing the pad of his thumb to my rear hole.

I quivered with the pleasure the sensation brought.

"You like that?" He pressed his thumb in deeper.

"Mmm, yes," I breathed.

He hooked an arm under my thigh and lifted my ass off the bed high enough to lightly lick my rear hole.

"Fuck, Frosty," Storm muttered.

Frost turned his face just far enough to grin at Storm before licking again. He replaced his tongue with his finger, pushing it deep inside me.

"Frost," I moaned. "I'm going to come."

"Of course you are," Storm said. "Because you're a good girl."

In Frost's cottage, I was a bad girl, but I liked being the good girl today. I wanted to please them. To do what they said. To do what Storm said.

I came hard and fast against Frost's mouth, with his finger deep inside my ass. Instead of being a million universes away, I was right here, feeling everything he was doing to me. Every touch, every lick. Everything.

I tipped my head back and cried out to the ceiling. The whole apartment building probably heard me, but I didn't give a shit. Let them hear. Let them know I was having a good time. Let them be jealous of us.

As I sagged back against the mattress, Frost lowered me down and rolled me over so I was lying on top of him, my legs straddling him. He grabbed my ass with his hands and positioned me over his cock.

I sat up a little, wriggling my hips to get into place before lowering myself down onto him.

"Dallas, how do you feel about anal?" Storm asked.

"Where's the lube?" Dallas replied.

With a slight laugh for his instant reply, I pointed to the table beside the bed. I didn't have to say a word before he was bouncing off and grabbing it out.

Faster than I would have thought was humanly possible, he had the lube open and was smearing a generous finger-full over my rear hole. He tossed the tube of lube aside on the bed and straddled Frost's legs.

He pressed a finger inside me, rolled it around slowly and carefully before inserting another and doing it again.

"You're so fucking tight," he breathed. "I'm already addicted to fucking you here." He slipped his fingers free and replaced them with his cock, easing himself into me, bit by bit. "So. Fucking. Tight."

"I can feel you," Frost said softly. "I can feel you inside her. It's... Holy shit."

"I can feel you too," Dallas said in awe. He slid halfway out of me, before pushing back in, always moving slowly and carefully, giving me a chance to stretch and get used to how thick he was.

"I can feel both of you," I whispered. I loved having two of them inside me at the same time. I glanced over at Storm. There was room for a third.

Taking the hint, he crawled over to me, took his cock between his thumb and forefinger and tapped it against my lips. "Be a good girl and open up."

I pretended to be stubborn for a moment, but then opened my mouth and took his cock in nice and deep. He filled my mouth the way the others filled my pussy and ass.

Then all three of them thrust into me, Dallas setting the pace for the other two. Sliding in and out of my ass while Frost thrust up into me. While Storm slowly fucked my mouth. While I inched closer to another orgasm.

"I'm going to come," Frost said, his face scrunched up in an effort to hold himself back.

"Yes, you are, because you're a good boy," Storm

told him. "Come inside her. You too, Dallas. Show our woman how fucking hot she is."

Dallas glanced over at him, frowning, but that didn't stop him from doing what he was told. He came at the same time Frost did, both with even, firm strokes into me as they shouted their releases and spilled themselves into my body.

Storm was only a handful of moments behind them, filling my mouth with his own salty, delicious cum.

All three sets of eyes were on me when he drew his cock out of my mouth and I was able to swallow.

"Good girl," Frost said. "Such a good fucking girl."

"She really is," Dallas agreed. "The best." he looked very much like he wanted to spend the day right where he was.

To be honest, I would have happily done the same. Let them lie there inside me until we all got too hungry to stay any longer.

Or at least, for a little while.

After a while, we all had to concede the need to get up and get to work.

I had a quick shower and breakfast and drove myself to the stadium for my last day of practical placement.

"It's been good having you around," Doctor Stuart said once we were done going over the treatment regimes for each of the injured players. None were too major. No doubt they were saving that for when the season began. The players all took things slightly easier during the preseason. Not to mention Coach didn't want his starting lineup badly injured at this time of the year. They sat out of a lot of the preseason games, giving the younger, newer players a chance to have a turn on the paddock.

That, I was glad for, but it still left question marks over my own head.

I winced. "That sounds final. Can I ask if Bruce said anything about me?"

"You can ask, but he hasn't." Doctor Stuart turned off his laptop and shut the lid. "He's been very close-mouthed about everything. Could be he hasn't made his mind up yet." He absently tapped his pointer finger on the desk beside his computer.

"I'm sure it's frustrating for you too," I said. "You need to know who you're working with."

"I do," he agreed. "I'm sure it'll be sorted out shortly. Bruce knows how important it is to have this put to bed as quickly as possible. So to speak." He added that without giving me a meaningful look, thank goodness. Innuendos from him would be awkward at best.

"Yeah." With the first game looming, it was going to be an urgent matter before too much longer. Bruce didn't seem like the kind of GM who'd risk the health of his players by taking too long to decide. By the same token, he wouldn't rush it either.

"Chin up," Doctor Stuart said. "Things will work out how they're supposed to. If that means you don't end up here, you'll find somewhere better."

"Doctor Anthony Stuart, are you suggesting there's a better team than the Dusk Bay Smashers?" I clicked my tongue.

"Watch your mouth, young woman." He shook his finger at me playfully. "I'd never suggest such a thing. Just that things will work out for you, that's all. You could end up working with the second best team in the league, the Sydney Devils."

"Don't say that to Atlas Underwood or Jay Lang," I said dryly. "I suspect both of them would strenuously disagree." I still needed to talk to Atlas about what happened the other day. The image of Jay's face, with his hurt eyes, kept flashing through my brain. I needed to know what the situation was between them, so I wouldn't make it worse.

Although, if it was as deep as Jay's expression implied, then wouldn't Atlas have said something? If I wasn't careful, the situation would give me a headache.

"They'll strenuously agree by the end of the season," Doctor Stuart said. "When the Smashers win the premiership."

"They'll have a hard time against the Chiefs," I said. "I've seen their lineup. They have some incredible players." And some large men. So did the Fijian team.

"Nothing we can't handle," Doctor Stuart said confidently. "Our boys are fit and ready to go. We'll live up to our name."

"Of course we... They..." I exhaled. I wanted to include myself, but I didn't dare to do that yet. In case I somehow jinxed myself.

Doctor Stuart raised an eyebrow. "If you don't get to work here, are you going to stop supporting the team?"

"Of course not," I said with a sniff. "We'll smash the rest of the teams. Happy now?"

He smiled. "Ecstatic. Not that I had any doubt

where your loyalties lay. You're with the grey and red, all the way."

"One hundred percent," I agreed. "I have all the hoodies, scarves and socks to prove it. Maybe that's what I did wrong. I should have worn them when I had my interview with Bruce Fergus. A scarf at least."

Doctor Stuart chuckled. "That might have been laying it on a bit thick. Although, a beanie might not have been a bad idea."

I slapped a hand to my forehead. "What was I thinking, going up there without wearing a knitted hat in the team colours? Talk about lack of foresight."

At least no one suggested I offer Bruce a blowjob in return for hiring me. If they did, I wouldn't have. That was something I would *not* want hanging over me for the rest of my career, even if it got me the job I wanted so much.

"I'm almost certain none of the other candidates wore one," Doctor Stuart said.

"They probably don't need to," I said with a sigh. "They have experience that would have spoken for itself."

"You have many qualities that make you perfect for the job," he assured me. "I know it's easy for me to say not to stress about it, but focus on the rest of the day and wait until you hear back from Bruce."

"You're right," I said. "I shouldn't let this interfere with work."

Maybe this was a test of some kind. If I let it distract me, then I'd fail.

"You're only human," Doctor Stuart said. "I'd be surprised if you weren't dwelling on this. I would be. In the meantime, we have a meeting with the team dietician. They need to make tweaks to a few of the guys' diets while they recover."

Every single aspect of their health and nutrition was under the microscope, all day every day. If *anything* changed, *everything* had to be considered. A few extra calories while they weren't as active as usual needed to be assessed. More of this, less of that, it was a science in itself.

I nodded. "After that, Atlas Underwood has an appointment to have his nose looked at." We needed to make sure it was healing right and not impeding his ability to breathe.

"I trust you can take care of that," Doctor Stuart said. "Fill me in on how it goes."

"Of course." I grabbed my phone and followed him into the infirmary's meeting room.

"How does it feel?" I looked at Atlas' nose from one side, then the other.

He shrugged. "It's fine. I'm still considering returning the favour."

"I don't think Coach would be too impressed if you broke Storm's nose on purpose." I leaned back and looked Atlas in the eyes. In the infirmary lighting, they looked brown-gold. Pretty enough to dive right into and get lost.

"Who said anything about doing it on purpose?" Atlas asked lightly. "Accidents happen." He gave me a sly smile.

"So you might accidentally have him fall on your fist?" I returned my attention to his nose.

"Or my knee," he agreed. "Or he might accidentally trip over my foot and faceplant into the wall. That would be *such* a shame."

"You realise none of that sounds accidental, right?" I asked, rolling my eyes at him. "I can't think of anyone who'd believe you if you said it was."

"Do I care if they believe me?" he shot back. "As long as no one can prove I did it on purpose."

"I don't think you're going to do any of that," I decided.

"You don't?" He cocked his head at me. "Why?"

"Because I think you're a better person than that," I told him. "You know Storm broke your nose by accident. Even if he did it on purpose, what would you gain by retaliating?"

"The satisfaction of hearing his bone crunch," Atlas said, drawing out the last word. "The possibility of wiping that smug look off his face for a day or two."

"What would it take for you to get along with each other?" I ended the question with a sigh.

"He'd have to stop being a prick, for a start." Atlas shrugged. "He needs to get over himself, especially where you're concerned. It didn't bother you did it? When I touched your neck?"

I glanced over my shoulder to make sure no one was listening. "It didn't bother me at all."

He leaned in closer and spoke with his mouth beside my ear. "I know. I felt your heart racing like a runaway train. You wanted it as much as I did."

"I did," I whispered. "What about Jay? Where does he fit into all of this?"

Atlas leaned back. "I don't know. It's complicated. He and I—" He shook his head.

"Are you together?" I asked.

"Not exactly," he said. "We've... Dabbled. I think he has feelings for me."

"He absolutely has feelings for you," I said. "Anyone could see that. Question is, do you have feelings for him?"

"Would it be a problem if I did?" He looked genuinely conflicted.

"Not at all," I said. "Not for me anyway. It might be a problem for him. He might prefer to keep you to himself."

Atlas took a couple of steps away and rubbed a hand over his stubbled chin. "I don't know if I want that. I want him and I want you."

He looked like he was going to add more, but didn't, so I had to ask. "What about Frost? You didn't seem to hate kissing him."

Atlas glanced around us, clearly uncomfortable with the topic, or at least the idea of being overheard.

I got that, guys like him often took longer to accept they had feelings for other men. Especially when those other men were teammates. A relationship could complicate things. A relationship breakdown could make being teammates difficult, to say the least. Not to mention the possibility of people pointing fingers and making judgements.

People needed to mind their own fucking business.

"I want to kiss you too," Atlas said. "I want to do more than kiss you. Can we— Can we have this conversation somewhere else?"

"Definitely. I need to have your nose x-rayed so I can see how it's healing. The technician should be ready." Doctor Stuart was right, I needed to focus on work. This wasn't the place for this conversation.

"Dinner?" Atlas asked before stepping towards the x-ray room.

"Sounds good," I agreed. We had a lot to talk about.

I waited while the technician took the x-ray, then looked at the pictures, comparing them to the ones taken on the day of the break.

"Admit it, you've never seen such sexy nose bones," Atlas said, peering over my shoulder.

"If I was ever going to call nose bones sexy, it would definitely be yours," I said with a laugh. "I mean, look at those boney bones."

"Would you say they're the boniest bones that ever boned?" He stepped around and grinned.

"I'd say they're right up there," I agreed. They looked like average nose bones to me, to be honest but I liked the way he smiled at the silly banter.

"All this talking about bones is giving me a boner," he whispered.

I laughed. "Serves you right for bringing up the topic." My gaze dipped to the front of his track pants. Light grey ones, which were helpful for displaying his growing erection.

"Ouch, thanks for the sympathy." He dropped his hands in front of his groin.

"I'm supposed to be treating your nose right now," I reminded him. "Which, by the way, is healing nicely. I don't think we'll have to amputate."

"That's fucking good," he said with a laugh. "I couldn't give you permission to amputate my nose." He leaned in and whispered, "But I give you permission to treat my cock, any time."

"I'm sure you do." I slipped the x-rays into a cardboard sleeve and printed out a sticker to identify who they belonged to.

"I'll pick you up at six," he said. "Wear something warm."

"Are we going to the beach again?" I asked. The weather had cooled off quickly, making it a bit chilly for sitting outside, even with a roaring fire.

"Not this time, but I'm not telling you where I'm taking you," he said. "Trust me, you'll have fun. And after that, we can talk about further treatment." He dipped his chin towards his groin and smiled.

"I'll see you later." I patted his shoulder and stepped away, leaving him with his hands still over his bulging tent. If this was my last day here, ever, at least it went out on an interesting note. I'd be thinking about him for the rest of the day. And how it would feel to ride his cock.

Chapter Twenty Two

Chelsea

"Who did you have to bribe for these seats?" I sat on the aisle, nothing between me and the stage but a metre or so of leg room.

Atlas grinned. "I didn't have to bribe anyone. I'm friends with the saxophonist, Jasper Wells. He lives a few doors down from me."

Given Jasper lived in the more opulent part of Dusk Bay, their houses probably weren't that close together. By 'house,' I mean 'huge house near the bay.' My brother lived up there too, in the house his boyfriend inherited from his late father.

"Of course you are," I said. "I didn't realise you were an Ice Blue Roses fan."

"From way back," he said. "Since before they were big. Jasper and I practically grew up together.

Funny how we both ended up here in the same city." His lips twisted to the side, clearly still not impressed at ending up with the Smashers.

"That is funny," I agreed. "Did it make coming here any easier?"

"Some," he said with a vague half-shrug. "He's the one who introduced me to Daze. I guess you could say the rest is history."

I cocked my head at him. "Did you ever think of saying no to her?"

"Not really. I like to live dangerously." He demonstrated that by dipping his hand into my tub of popcorn.

"People have lost body parts doing that," I said.

He grinned and shoved the popcorn into his mouth. "No idea what you're talking about. I'm as pure as hell. As innocent as anyone else here in Dusk Bay."

"I don't think that's saying much, considering." Innocent and Dusk Bay didn't go together very well. Or at all.

"You wouldn't really hurt me for stealing your popcorn, would you?" he asked. "You might find my hands useful." He placed one of them on my thigh.

"I'll think about it." I leaned over and stole a

handful of his popcorn. Smiling at him with my eyes, I shoved it into my mouth.

"I think that makes us even," he said.

"I think so," I agreed. "But keep your hands out of my popcorn." I shook a finger at him.

"Or what?" he asked. "Do I seem like the kind of guy who follows the rules?" He wiggled his eyebrows at me.

"To some extent," I said slowly. "You wouldn't be a professional rugby player if you couldn't follow the rules *some* of the time."

He made a face. "Okay, you got me. Sometimes I follow rules. Off the field though, that's a different story."

"You'll have to tell me some time," I said. The seats around us were filling quickly, and the arena was getting louder. I wanted to ask what he did for Daze, but that would have to wait until after the concert.

"Hey, dickhead."

I whipped my head around to see Jasper Wells had stopped beside us. He offered Atlas a fist bump.

"Hey, asshole." Atlas leaned past me to bump fists with the saxophone player. "Shouldn't you be warming up?"

Jasper ignored him and turned his gaze to me. "Did you lose a bet? That's the only reason I can think of for a woman to go out with a reprobate like Atlas Underwood here." He smiled and gave me a wink.

"Fuck off, Wells," Atlas said on a laugh. "She's here voluntarily. Because she has excellent taste."

"If you say so. She looks smart enough to figure you out for herself." To me, he added, "When you figure him out, get him to give you my number. I'll show you a better time than he ever could." No one would ever accuse Jasper of being humble, including him.

My face actually heated. It wasn't every day I had a conversation with a rock star, much less have them flirt with me.

"I'll keep that in mind," I said. As if I didn't already have my hands full. Otherwise, I might consider adding him to my growing group of guys. If he'd go along with that.

"There's no way in hell I'd give her your number," Atlas said. "Chelsea is too good for a prick like you."

"I think that's up to Chelsea, don't you?" Jasper asked. "Maybe I should give it to her myself."

"Not if you need all of your fingers to play," Atlas growled.

Jasper leaned down and spoke to me. "How adorable is that? He's actually trying to threaten me."

"I noticed that," I said. I had to admit Jasper smelled good, a combination of leather from his jacket and soap. "I'm sure he'd never act on it."

Daze wouldn't be impressed if two of the guys who worked for her started trying to remove each other's fingers. That was usually reserved for the enemy. Or anyone who stole from her or the people she worked for.

"Not unless he gives me good reason," Atlas said. "Which he won't, because Jasper is a dickhead, but he's not going to muscle in on another guy's date."

"I would, but I have to go and warm up." Jasper leaned in even further, close enough to whisper in my ear. "Think of me when you're fucking him." He gave me another wink before straightening up and heading up to the stage.

A ripple of surprise and excitement passed through the audience. They must not have realised he was talking to us until he left. Just as well, or security would be busy stopping him from getting mobbed.

I turned to Atlas and raised my eyebrows at him.

He frowned. "What?"

"You two are like brothers," I said. "I bet you give each other hell, but you actually like each other."

"He's the brother I never had," Atlas said easily. "When I called him and asked for tickets, he was happy to give us these. He's a grumpy prick, but he's a good guy deep down. Mostly. He would totally have taken you backstage and fucked you if you let him, even though you're here with me."

"I'm shocked a rock star would behave that way," I said sarcastically.

Atlas snorted. "I know, right? He's such a horn-dog. No doubt he'll have a party with a few of the groupies after the concert. The whole band will."

"What's the point of being a rock star if you can't have fun with your fans?" I asked. If I was a rock star, I'd fuck groupies left and right too.

"Good point," Atlas said.

"I'm sure you've had your share of ruck bunnies," I said.

"And then some," he agreed. "After a while, it becomes a blur."

I could relate to that. My clients at Flirts became a blur too after the first few weeks. Every now and again, one would stand out, like Storm, Frost and Dallas, but the rest had faded from my memory.

"What are you thinking about?" Atlas asked.

"Maybe I should tell you about it after the concert," I said. I didn't want to ruin a fun evening with the reality of my past.

He sat around to face me and lightly touched my forehead with his. "How about you tell me now. It looked important."

"It— I suppose it kind of is," I agreed.

"Go ahead, I'm listening," he insisted.

I opened my mouth and the words came out in a rush. "Until recently, I used to be an exotic dancer."

"Exotic..." He pulled back and stared at me, a frown creasing his brow. "As in..."

"I took my clothes off for money," I said. "And had sex for money."

The roar of the crowd had lessened compared to the roar of blood in my ears. I hadn't expected to have this conversation with him like this. Not in the front row, waiting for a rock concert to start.

"I see," he said simply. "You said 'until recently.' You don't do it anymore?"

I shook my head. "It was only to put myself through university. A girl has to eat."

My laugh was nervous. I couldn't tell what he

was thinking. I wasn't sure he knew yet either. He was still trying to process what I said.

"Right. I suppose she does." He sat back in his chair. His body was rigid, jaw clenched tighter than Storm's ever was. That was the only sign he was trying to contain himself. He was using his on-field discipline to keep from losing his shit.

"I would have said something sooner, but it's an awkward topic to bring up," I said.

My palms started to sweat. I shouldn't have said anything to him here. I should have insisted we wait until we were alone, somewhere else. Would that have been better? He might have responded the same, but it wouldn't have been so public. I felt as though everyone was watching me, even though I knew they weren't. Their attention was all on the stage. Where ours should be.

"I'll say," he agreed. "Do the other guys know?"

"They do," I said. I decided not to elaborate on that right now. If he was going to judge me for what I did, he'd likely judge them for frequenting Flirts.

"Okay," he said slowly. That seemed to irritate him even more. It wasn't just me keeping secrets from him, it was them as well. It must be annoying the hell out of him to realise Storm knew, and he didn't.

"Only them, not the team as a whole," I said quickly.

"Okay," he said again. "Let's just enjoy the concert."

"Yeah." That sounded final to me. Like he was disgusted to learn about my old life. Apparently it was okay for him to fuck footy fans, but not for me to fuck for money. "If the team finds out…"

He turned his face to regard me. His golden brown eyes were deep and dark, betraying nothing but simmering anger. Who was it aimed at? I couldn't be certain. Me for my past? Him for not somehow knowing? The other guys for knowing already? Maybe all of those. Or maybe something else. Perhaps the understanding that being seen with me could be detrimental to his career.

"I'm sure it won't be pretty," he said finally.

"I'm sure it won't," I agreed. "I should leave." If I was gone before people started taking photos of him, or asking for selfies, it might lessen the impact on his future. He could pretend the only dealings we ever had was professional, as his doctor. He could distance himself from me and any scandal that might arise.

Honestly, that was a sensible approach for him to take, although the idea of it stung.

That was selfish of me, I decided. There was a lot more at stake than my feelings, my ego. Not just his future, but the future of the team. I was insignificant in comparison. I blinked away the moisture that threatened to spill down my cheeks.

One hand on the arm of my chair, I started to push myself to my feet. Before I could take a step away, he grabbed my wrist and pulled me back down.

"I said, let's enjoy the concert," he said so quietly I almost missed hearing him over the crowd. "We can talk afterwards." His gaze bore into mine, quiet determination that I should do what he said. Along with that, an underlying threat of what he might do to me if I disobeyed. It wasn't the threat of being stripped and spanked, it was something far worse than that. I might be the next body in the cemetery beside Ivy.

His hands rested in his lap, but his fingers were curled like he was picturing wrapping them around my neck.

My tongue darted over my lips. I didn't like being told what to do. I certainly didn't like to be threatened, there was something about him that suggested it wasn't a threat. He could get to me and destroy me long before anyone who cared about me could stop him. He wasn't scared of the potential retaliation. If anything, he was facing it down.

I nodded and sank back into my seat. Enjoying myself might be a big ask, but I'd stay.

What choice did I have?

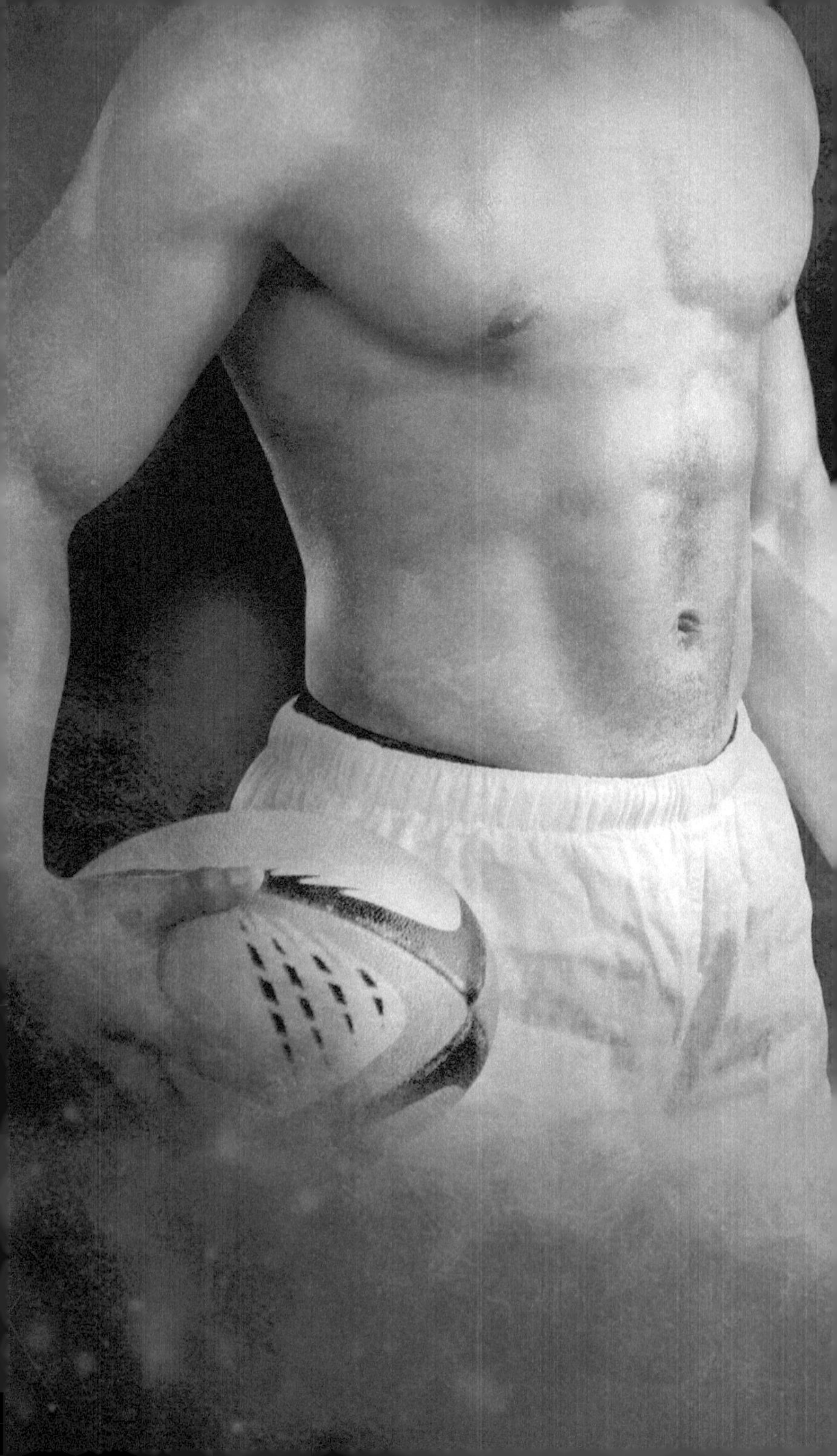

Chapter Twenty Three

Chelsea

I WOULD HAVE ENJOYED THE CONCERT A LOT more if I wasn't watching Atlas out of the corner of my eye the entire time. He grooved, clapped and sang along with everyone else in the audience, as though he forgot our conversation already. He looked like nothing more than a rugby god, out to enjoy himself at a rock concert. He even knew every single word of every single song, even the new stuff.

Jasper only appeared on stage a handful of times, playing the saxophone and occasionally winking at me or another woman in the audience. The lead singer, Decker Bolden, was just as flirty, clasping hands with various women and taking their phones to take photos of himself. The crowd loved every minute of it.

I just pretended to.

When the band finished their final encore, I shuffled out behind everyone else, Atlas on my heels.

He placed a hand on my shoulder and held me there as he said, "That wasn't so bad, was it?"

"It was...fun," I said awkwardly.

His fingers tightened on my skin. "If they ever need a backing dancer, I know where they can find one. If you can dance and keep your clothes on."

Fortunately the arena was still loud enough that only I heard him say that.

I looked at him over my shoulder. "I'll stick to medicine. That's what I do best."

He snorted, his breath brushing my neck. "I bet that's not true. Anyone who gets paid to fuck must be good at it."

I stiffened. "I'm very good at it." I brushed off his hand and hurried up the steps leading out of the arena.

He strode along behind me, keeping pace. When he followed me into the foyer, he was stopped by a couple of women a few years younger than both of us.

"Atlas Underwood!" one squealed. "You're even better looking in person. Can I get a selfie with you?"

"Of course," he said without glancing at me. His attention was all on her and her friend.

"I need to go to the bathroom," I said.

I did, but it would also be a good way to slip away from him and any watchful eyes. Even if I had to climb out the window. That was a last resort, but the longer I was with him, the uneasier I became. He was as volatile as Storm. Better to sneak away before things went south.

"Stay," was all Atlas said without taking his eyes off the women. He stood between them and smiled warmly at the phone in the first woman's hand. That was quickly replaced by the other woman's phone and more smiles.

"Thank you so much!" Both women squealed now. "We're going to Hazards for a drink. Are you *coming?*"

I doubted anyone missed the emphasis on that last word. It was obviously an invitation to fuck one or both of them. Divina would have remarked they both had the perfect mouths for giving blowjobs. She would probably have offered them a job on the spot. What would they say to an offer like that? I suspected they'd decline.

"I might be along a bit later," he said. "Go ahead and start without me."

They pouted but walked away, hips swaying. One of them actually glanced back and gave him an air kiss before disappearing in the throng. Neither of them seemed to have noticed I existed, or cared. If they thought we were together, they still would have made the offer.

His obvious hypocrisy annoyed the hell out of me. He didn't like it when Jasper came on to me before the concert, but it was okay for those women to come on to him? If that was how he was, I'd be better off without him.

"Maybe you should go," I said. He might enjoy spending time with them instead of me. Women like that might be more his type. A quick fuck with no complications. Honestly, that didn't sound too bad right now.

"We're not done," he said. "Come with me." He took my hand, lacing his fingers in mine and guided me out the big glass doors at the front of the arena. He walked beside me like we were nothing more interesting than a couple out on a pleasant date, enjoying the concert and then the night air. Maybe later we'd go home, bake some cupcakes and have vanilla sex.

"I know you must have been surprised," I started.

That was an understatement. He was obviously a lot more than surprised.

He glanced around, uneasy eyes scanning the crowd to see if anyone was paying us any attention. A couple of people glanced at him, but most seemed in a hurry to get away from the arena. To reach their cars, or a bar where they could enjoy a few drinks.

"Not here." We walked a couple of blocks until we reached a quieter part of the city. We weren't completely alone, but we were away from the thickest of the crowds. If he decided to kill me, he'd have an audience. And so would I. But we were far enough away from anyone else that we could talk and not be overheard. Not unless things got heated and loud.

Finally done with waiting, I stopped, pulling him to a halt with me. "I don't regret what I did. I needed to work. That's all there was to it."

He let go of my hand and placed his on the wall behind me, pinning me in.

"I had to work before I turned professional. Do you know what I did? I delivered pizza. I had a shitty little car that I used to drive around Sydney, delivering fucking *pizza*. Later on, it was on the back of a bike. Dodging in and out of city traffic, trying not to get killed to bring people their hot *fucking* meals.

Never once did it occur to me to take my clothes off or fuck strangers. Not once."

"Funny, it never occurred to me to deliver food on the back of a bike," I said tartly.

I would have preferred to work in a restaurant, carrying food to tables. Or behind a bar, pouring drinks, side by side with Sadie. "I danced because I was good at it. Because the money was good. And guess what? Because I enjoyed it. And I was much less likely to be hit by a car while spinning around a pole." The job wasn't without its risks, but I never had to worry about getting run over.

"No, you had strangers staring at your body," he hissed. "Leering at you and getting turned on."

I cocked my head at him. "Judging by those women who wanted selfies with you, that's exactly how they see you when you're out on the field playing."

"It's not the same thing," he snarled. "I'm out there playing football, not baring my tits. Not spreading my legs for fuck only knows who."

"Is that the problem?" I asked calmly. "Are you jealous? Do you wish you were the one I was spreading my legs for? Or is this one of those 'women shouldn't behave like that' things?"

"It's—" He closed his eyes and shook his head

before shoving himself off the wall and taking a few steps away. "I don't know. If it was one of my sisters, I'd want to rip out their eyeballs."

"I'm not your sister," I pointed out. "But if any of them wanted to dance, I'd support them even if you don't. Because, guess what? Women get to make decisions about what they do with their own bodies. If I wanted to take my clothes off here in the street, I could." I might get arrested for it, but I could still do it.

He ran a hand over the back of his head. "Fuck. I *know* that. I just hate the idea of you doing it."

"No shit," I said dryly. "I think this is something you need to think about and come to terms with. If you can't do that, I guess that's that."

"I don't know if I can," he said. "I don't know if I can get my head around it. If the team finds out…"

"Is that the actual problem?" I asked. "If they find out, I'd be screwed. You're worried I'd take you down with me."

"Wouldn't you?" he asked evenly. "How would this look?" He raised his hands to either side before dropping them to his thighs with a slap.

"I offered to leave the concert," I pointed out. "You were the one who insisted I stay."

"People would have noticed if you walked out on

me," he said. "They would have started speculating. If they start looking into you, how difficult would it be to find out what you used to do?"

"Someone already did," I said. In as few words as possible, I told him about Belinda Simmons and what happened to her.

"This just gets better and better," he said sarcastically. "Let's just kill everyone who digs into your past. And here you are, trying to get a job in a high-profile situation. Why?"

"Because I don't think being a dancer should have any bearing on anything else in my life," I said. "I'm a good doctor. I'd work hard for the team. Why should a past job prevent me from doing that? That's as ridiculous as suggesting delivering pizzas should stop you from playing rugby. A job is a job. That's all I see it as. Would you have preferred I do a job like Belinda Simmons? Follow people like you around and wait for an opportunity to take an embarrassing photo? To dig into your personal life and that of your family? Maybe I could have exposed some deep, dark secret one of your sisters has. Or I could expose to the world the fact you work with people like Daisy Lasalle. How well do you think that will go down if the team finds out?"

"As far as anyone knows, they're just businesspeople," he replied sharply. "Friends I do favours for."

"Have you killed for them?" I asked. "Broken a few bones? Maybe a finger or two? Or a kneecap?"

He averted his gaze. "I haven't killed anyone. Yet."

"You're not denying the rest of it," I pointed out. "What I did, it never hurt anyone. Quite the opposite. I entertained them, just like you do out on the football field. Just like Ice Blue Roses did for us in there." I waved roughly in the direction of the arena. "It's not different just because you say it is. Just because you're uncomfortable with the idea of other men looking at my body. You know Storm looks at me, right? And Frost. And Dallas. Do you have a problem with that?"

"They're not paying you for it," he said.

"Not now they're not," I said quietly. I watched as my words sank in.

"They—" He gaped at me. "Fuck."

"Yeah, fuck," I said. "As meet cutes go, it was a little different. But it doesn't change things between us. This shouldn't change things between you and me either. But that's something you have to decide for yourself. I like you, but if you can't deal with my past, I'll do my best to stay out of your way."

"You're not working with the team," he stated quietly.

"I haven't heard back from the GM about my interview," I said. "It's possible I'm not."

"That'll make it easier to stay out of my way," he said. "I can't see you if you're not there."

"Not unless I get the job," I said.

He gave me a look like if he had his way, that was out of the question. Without another word, he turned and walked away.

Chapter Twenty Four

Frost

"He did *what*?" Storm's face was a fascinating shade of pissed off. If he was a cartoon character, he'd have steam coming out of his ears.

"Nothing yet," Chelsea said. "He freaked out. It happens." She sat cross-legged on the couch, both hands curled around a cup of coffee.

"It's the 'yet' I'm worried about," Storm said. "You got the impression he was going to insist the GM not hire you? What kind of bullshit is that?" His gaze flicked over to me. It wasn't that long ago we considered asking for the same thing. That Chelsea not work for the team. At the time, that was to keep her away from guys like Atlas. It might not have been such a bad idea after all.

"He was just reacting." She looked down into her coffee.

"I'll react back at him," Storm snapped. "With my fist."

"I'd help if that would change anything," Dallas said. "It won't. It'll make things worse."

"It'll make me feel better," Storm said. He stomped away towards the window and stood looking out, silent for a while.

I moved over to sit beside Chelsea. "You okay?"

She shrugged. "I got a front row ticket to Ice Blue Roses. I should be grateful for that."

"Doesn't sound worth it to me," I said. "If you didn't get to enjoy it because of him."

"I shouldn't have said anything." She sighed, making her coffee ripple.

"Of course you should," I said. "It's part of your life. If he cared about you, he'd understand that."

"It's not that simple," she said. "Do you ever wonder what would happen to you if the team found out what I did and connected you to me? What it would do to your career? All of your careers. Maybe he was right to walk away. It might be better for everyone if you walked away from me too."

"I don't care what they say about me," I said. "I'm

not leaving you. You're stuck with me, whether you like it or not."

"Me too," Dallas said. "If the team doesn't like it, they can fuck off."

"You say that now, but if it happened, it wouldn't be that simple," she said. "You love rugby. You have years left to play."

"Exactly," I said. "Only years. We have decades left to be with you. Seems like a no-brainer to me." She was right in one regard. I wanted to retire from playing when I was ready, not under a cloud of scandal.

"If I don't work for the team, no one has any reason to go digging into my past," she said slowly. "I could work at the hospital, or one of the GP clinics in town."

Storm turned around and leaned his back against the wall. "That would be like spending years trying to get signed by a team, then working in the supermarket stacking shelves instead."

"I used to stack shelves in the supermarket," I pointed out.

"Yeah, but you didn't choose it instead of playing rugby." Storm cocked his head at me, his anger having simmered down somewhat.

"No," I agreed. "Some days, when Coach has us

training hard, I wondered if I made the right life choice." I smiled, hoping to get one out of Chelsea. I hated to see her so bummed. Especially over Atlas. Of all the guys, he was the one I would have guessed would understand why she used to dance.

"I'm sure you did," she said. "Which is why I need to make the right choice now. I'll contact the GM in the morning and withdraw my application." Tears glistened on her lashes.

"You will not," Storm said. "You belong with the team."

"I agree with him," Dallas said. "We want you there, working at the stadium. Travelling with us."

"Close by when Dallas needs to get off," I teased.

He looked at me evenly and nodded. "That too."

I shook my head at him, indulgently, then turned back to Chelsea. "I want you there too. We can deal with whatever happens. For all we know, Atlas will feel different in the morning. Or in a few days. If you walk away from the job now, it might be for nothing."

"It might be, and it might prevent a shit storm," she said. "I don't want any of you caught in the middle of that."

"We could deal with Atlas, if that would help," I offered.

"Don't," she said firmly. "That would upset Daze. Believe me, you don't want to do that."

"I don't want you upset." I put a hand over one of hers. "I love you, I want you to be happy."

She smiled faintly. "I want to be happy too, but me being upset doesn't usually end up with people dying."

"Usually," I said teasingly. "If Atlas is going to make life difficult for you—"

"Don't kill Atlas," she said. "Promise me." Her blue eyes were firm.

"I won't kill him unless I have to," I said. I didn't want to kill him, not really. I did want to find out what the hell was going on in his head though. Could he come around to understand? It wasn't that big a deal, was it?

Her gaze lingered on my face, but finally she nodded. She also understood we didn't know what the future held. I might, some day, find myself in a circumstance where I had no choice. If that was the case, making a promise to her now, might mean making a promise I'd have to break. I never wanted to do that to her. Not if I could help it.

"I don't promise not to punch him in the face," Storm said. "I told you he was an asshole. Once an asshole, always an asshole."

Chelsea swivelled around. "Don't do anything rash. Give him some time to think about things. He knows it's not in the team's best interests for him to go public with this. Once he calms down, he'll realise my dancing wasn't a big deal."

"And if he doesn't?" Dallas asked.

"Then we'll handle whatever happens," she said. "If that means I walk away from the team, then so be it. I don't want you to be rash and I won't be either. Let's give it a little while and see what happens. Okay?"

"Okay," I said. "I could try to talk to him. See where his head is at."

"It might be a good idea to leave him alone for now," she said after a few moments thought. She glanced down into her coffee which must be getting cold by now.

"What is it?" I asked.

"This wasn't how I hoped the night would go," she said.

"At least you have us," I said. "We won't walk away from you or let you down."

She looked up and smiled. "I know you won't. You three are amazing. I'm grateful to have you in my life."

"Not as grateful as we are," Dallas said. He leaned forward to squeeze her knee.

"What they said," Storm said gruffly. He still looked ready to rearrange Atlas' face, but he'd keep his temper in check for now. At least until he saw Atlas again. I had a feeling things might get ugly then, regardless of any promises he made now.

"Let us show you," I said softly. I took the cup from her hands and placed it on the coffee table. I helped her to her feet and, without warning, scooped her up in my arms and carried her into her bedroom.

Chelsea

I woke slowly. Surrounded by three warm, muscular bodies. I didn't want to move, but I had to get up and use the toilet. I grabbed some clothes on the way. Frost's track pants and Dallas' T-shirt. I squirmed into them and headed into the kitchen to start making breakfast and coffee.

While the kettle started to boil, I took my phone off the charge and glanced at the screen. The blood drained from my face.

"What is it? You look like you've seen a ghost."

I hadn't seen Frost enter the kitchen until he spoke.

"It's Bruce Fergus, the GM," I said slowly.

"He wants to see you?" Frost asked.

"No." I looked up at him and shook my head. "He's dead."

Thank you for reading! The story continues in Twisted Ruck. For a bonus CNC scene from Chelsea's point of view, you can claim yours here.

About the Author

Maggie Alabaster writes reverse harem romance.

She lives in NSW, Australia with one spouse, two daughters, one dog, and countless birds.

Sign up for Maggie's newsletter! Sign Up!

Join Maggie's reader group! Join here!

Follow Maggie on Bookbub! Click here to follow me!

Check out Maggie's website- www.maggiealabaster.com

Also by Maggie Alabaster

Ruck Boys

Filthy Ruck

Hard Ruck

Twisted Ruck

Bad Ruck

Dirty Ruck

Deadly Ruck

Sparrow and the Mafia Kings

Possessive

Ruined

Corrupted

Pucking Dark Hearts

Pucking Hearts Collide

Pucking Forbidden Hearts

Pucking Hardened Hearts

Dusk Bay Demons

Puck Drop

Breakaway

Power Play

Brutal Academy

Book 1 Heartless

Book 2 Cruel

Book 3 Vengeful

Court of Blood and Binding

Book 1 Song of Scent and Magic

Book 2 Crown of Mist and Heat

Book 3 Sword of Balm and Shadow

Book 4 Whisper of Frost and Flame

Dark Masque

Book 1 Bait

Book 2 Prey

Book 3 Trap

Saving Abbie

Book 1 Pitch

Book 2 Pound

Book 3 Session

Book 4 Muse

Book 5 Rhythm

Book 6 Encore

Novella Venomous

Saving Abbie books 1-4

Saving Abbie books 4-6 + Venomous

Ruthless Claws

Book 1 Ivory

Book 2 Crimson

Book 3 Elodie

Harmony's Magic

Book 1 Summoned by Fire

Book 2 Summoned by Fate

Book 3 Summoned by Desire

Shifter's Vault

Book 1 Discarded

Book 2 Deceived

Book 3 Disgraced

My Alien Mates

Book 1 Star Warriors

Book 2 Star Defenders

Book 3 Star Protectors

Academy of Modern Magic

Book 1 Digital Magic

Book 2 Virtual Magic

Book 3 Logical Magic

Complete Collection

Summer's Harem

Book 1: Shimmer

Book 2: Glimmer

Book 3: Flicker

Complete collection

Short reads

Taken by the Snowmen

Jingle All the Way

Also by Maggie Alabaster and Erin Yoshikawa

Caught by the Tide

Book 1 –Pursued by Shadows

Book 2 Pursued by Darkness

Book 3 Pursued by Monsters